SDP
— SWEAT DRENCHED PRESS —

N. CASIO POE

PIECEMEAL: THE FINAL CUT

Copyright 2022 © N. Casio Poe

&

Copyright 2022 © Sweat Drenched Press

INTRODUCTION Copyright 2022 © Zak Ferguson

& Sweat Drenched Press.

All rights reserved. This book or any portion thereof may not be reproduced or used in any manner whatsoever without the express written permission of the publisher or writer except for the use of brief quotations in a book review or article.

Cover art by N. Casio Poe

Paperback Version **ISBN:** 9798387860461

This is a work of fiction. Names and characters are the product of the authors imagination and any resemblances.

PIECEMEAL: THE FINAL CUT

N. CASIO POE

N. CASIO POE

INTRODUCTION:

PIECEMEAL: *The Final Cut* is a further evolved variation of the original piece. A solid piece it was. But, it seems fitting that a film/graphic novel/music/merchandise/book/toy-fanatic like *N. Casio Poe* should have a deluxe version put out, or a different cut of his seminal novel.

I was with this book from the start of its publication history, *way back when*. I witnessed it being put out into the world and though I had little hand in its overall edit and final look and feel I was very keen on it, when I first read it as a manuscript, back in a day when I was associated with a now **long gone** publication house.

N. Casio writes with a passion, a temper, but also with tongue-firmly--in-cheek. Saturated in bodily juices and violence and mania he is a writer that has a perpetual middle-finger held aloft to those he deems below himself – (*it must take a long time to type his works out if he does that throughout the writing process, I must tell you*) in, less rebellion, but more in retaliation.

Poe's work challenges you to swallow your inhibitions and tolerances and tastes. A lump that throughout reading his works you just can't quite *swallow*. Though, we secretly love harsh, drastic, volatile art, we also love pushing the envelope, in various forms, typographically and grammatically. As writers/artists that write within the realms of the niche, the real underground it is par for the course. Those that truly invest and get taken away by this are the readers, themselves. You want to get a close to that realm, that world, that seedy, disgusting, lewd, deranged arena, as much as possible without

PEACEMEAL: THE **FINAL** CUT

adverse consequences, you perverted bunch of sickos. Supping on depraved works such as Poe's.

It is like cum being forced down your throat, whilst the cum-shooter himself is laughing at you, frothing from the mouth, poking you in the ribs with his even frothier cock - you kind of end up enjoying the whole perverted nature of it.

As an individual I do not fit into people's boxes nor does my own work and nor does N's.

That is what so appeals to me and many readers.

There is no wall he won't climb over to witness something off, no war-torn plane he won't rush into, not paying mind to the torn-asunder soldiers telling him to "Go back!" delighting in the fireworks and limbs flying - there is no BDSM brothel or Toy Store or Flea Market he won't cruise and study and collect.

His nonchalance in the anarchy and the madness being just second nature is also what is so addictive. His approach and attitude. He also isn't deluded. I have heard many podcasts where supposed "twansgwessive!" writer's opened up as to how hard this transgressive piece of literature was, all whilst Poe is smashing out 500 pages of filth and not losing a wink of sleep over any of it. Whether imagined by his own sickened mind or what is actually in existence in our sordid world.

His work is extremely violent, manic, anarchic, pop-culturally savvy and satirical. I love the ferocity of it all.

I love how attuned I am to the deliberateness to his grammatical/punctuational disregard.

An aesthetic is very much being created here. An almost sub-genre. A meta-verse where those who want to go into the dark web, but are too pussy to

- (I know I am, and I would never ever attempt it)- can!

But, that's the rush of it all, isn't it?

The dislocation and acceptability of it, by it being merely **F I C T I O N**.

That and those who love toy-brands and their history and love the whole angle of online internet trolls and Right-Wing-Propagandists and INCELS, will get a kick out of N. Casio's on point, hilariously far-too-close-to-the-bone take on it all.

Sweat Drenched Press is as always honoured to put out innovative, challenging reads. And N Casio Poe fits that bill, and then some. What I especially like is Casio's CRINGE MYTHOS is now under one banner. Under one Press. A rightful home.

N. Casio's works are unprecedentedly demented, cruel, silly, ferocious, darkly humorous. So, when N mentioned *PIECEMEAL* was up for grabs, I eventually enquired to its fate. As per, N agreed, and now here we have it. I am now part of its current state, like most of N Casio's work.

And to celebrate its re-release it will be put out as a lush deluxe edition HARDCOVER - Ooooooo, get us!

Sweat Drenched Press has now published five of N. Casio Poe's novels. And we will not stop.

Why? Because they're fucking good. *Really, really* good. They're what I'd call *Peter Sotos*-but-cheaper. Sotos is a pornographer, who deals with unnerving material, and is a niche, with a dedicated fanbase, perhaps Poe is one of them too; but, his work is so *niche*, that his books are **expensive**.

For me, far too expensive. Whereas *Sotos* is all about shock value, perversity, depravity, Poe isn't. Poe is pulp. He is extreme. He is modern. Post-modern. Anti-post-modern. There is so much going on between the cock-sucking, anus-dribbling and strange serial-killing miasmas of ill-intent and obsession, that I feel he far exceeds the levels of *Peter Sotos*.

His works pack a brutal, unnerving, disgusting punch, that you feel dirty reading; but, you are also entertained, thrust into a vastly mapped out world – rich, vibrant, often sometimes far too compelling as I thought half the stuff he wrote about existed, more fool me, aye?

He is a prosaist *enfant terrible* in the REAL HARDCORE sense. His is the thinkers' version of *Peter Sotos*.

His is the savvy and pop culturally saturated *Sotos*. Like most books by N. Casio Poe, I have a real fondness and like.

And I hope you do too, dear reader, holding this new SWEAT DRENCHED CLASSICS EDITION?

You better.

A lot of work goes into Poe's work, and I feel it deserves a greater, wider, audience, than it has.

– Zak Ferguson (Author & Co-Founder of SDP) 2022

N. CASIO POE

PIECEMEAL:

```
THE FINAL CUT

N. CASIO POE
```

"Of all the strictures ever being wound over the impulse to create, the pathologically sociopathic need to be relatable is both the most egregious and debilitating"

from the journals of Karigan Stello.

no date.

PEACEMEAL: THE FINAL CUT

Raw materials. Little more than a compiling of raw materials not even condescending to a narrative tether. Under the naive impression that you were offering "nightmares to discriminating readers", which as I interpret mean writing that is free from the conventions that serve only to inhibit the terrors within, "narrative" being the most egregious of those conventions. To apply a narrative to these writings would rob them of their purpose; capturing ugliness in as accurate a fashion as the form would allow.

This is not about telling a story. Not about character arcs.

This is about exploration of subconscious terrains. Inhabiting parallel universe.

The parts I search for in all my varying consumptions.
Prurient feeds to satiate my innate curiosities.

I've played your shit games.

Coprophagia fueled ascensions of pig-heap trivialities.

Calendar of menstruations masquerading as unflinching profundity.

Trust fund star gazing prescribed as "surrealism".

The developmentally arrested, sporadically peppering their trite fantasia of princes and princesses with soft bore pornography. When it's the menstruation itself that holds my attention, not the callow strictures of your limited imagination that only serves to inhibit its luminous viscosity.

The scarlet so dark, it's almost rectal.

The chewable gobs. The stiff odour.

Fuck your mood. Fuck your cramps.

Perhaps I should say fuck the interminable waterheads who condition you to think diaries say more about your mood and cramps than the mood and cramps say for themselves. Doubled over and betrayed by heart and brain seemingly by the minute. There's *your* power. Capture that. Save your soaked rotting pads. Staple them around the office. Make sandwiches out of them. Eat your biology.

I'll fuck on a period. The blood on my cock gives the impression of a conqueror worm. Shit has a similar effect on a cock. Something normally rejected by the body being scraped out by an invading force. Illusions of rape.

Some guys don't like that. Weaklings.

There's no other word for them. Certainly not "Faggot".

Can't imagine faggots are put off by blood and shit on their cocks. I still remember that first great anal sex experience. How hard I came and how after I pulled my cock out of her ass and saw traces of her meat-churned feces specking my cock that I almost came again. Revisit in my memories when I need to masturbate, but the hard-drive just won't do.

Asunder. Bruise knees blown from slipping on ice in parking lot. Screen grab of abused children shedding light on church paedophile ring. Cables held on ceiling with staples. 2 inch thick drinking glass ridged with tiny pyramids and half blades like shudders. Purple aroma sticks. Welts widening like blubber gash. Pressure, fear, or expectation justify, temper, and excuse. Interrogation values. Documents the countless abuses. Comprehensive excruciating detail. Sufficient inaccuracies. Forming a finger fuck centipede with the stars of a popular comedy series on the showroom floor of a Service Merchandise.

FRESH ADDENDUM:

The preceding compiled texts were recovered from a deleted post on the "Read the Red Room" forum on SadeExistance.com, believed to have been authored by failed mass shooter RAND PROUSHAYTHE, or at least someone using his message board handle; BLACKPILLAR13. The profile was quickly banned after PROUSHATHE's attempt on the life of NY congresswoman (now current Vice President) SALOME THRILWELL, which caused him to become a folk hero among right wing extremist circles, particular the SECTARIAN KARNAGE AXIS (SKA), who have continued to actively raise funds for PROUSHAYTHE's release and freedom... though rumors suggest the campaign is little more than a slush fund for their literary and cinematic propaganda materials; which have conveniently increased in production value since the PROUSHAYTHE fundraising campaign was launched.

LVV:

Billowing softy. Snapped two of ten digits at roots; one completely forward and other completely back. Hooks of bone crack skin. Fell to floor. Knees crashed. Wrapping fingers of other hand around wrist of mutilated twin. Bubbles and pops. Boiling water. Pot whistle to scream. Curled up. Back to stove door. knees hidden in brittle paper like fabric of black dress. Hysterically inhaling and exhaling. Snot lumping in back of nose. Trickling down throat. Baptizing cries with phlegm. Olive-green oven mitt picked up teapot. Glass of lid fogged.

Beads of condensation dripping along rim. Hair parted down middle. Color of hay. Took off lid. Dumped boiling water where hair parted. Baritone feminine growl out of mouth. Made fetus of self. Praying atmosphere would sheath over person as a faux uterus…

….shaving cream gathers in clumps in thistles below chin and cheeks. Follicle chinstrap. Coarse mustache needle scraping pig fat lip. Constant irritation making pink swollen. Oozing venom pout. Steam from pool. Pulverized by faucet. Spurting muddy chunks. Liver-spot stars on yellow porcelain. Face inked. Pen streaked black rain over bland marble. Artificial details mask uneventful features. Reflection and flesh collide. Spit spatters on mirror. Light green mucus. Chalk outline of insect homicide. Face stretches in mucus drip. Heated cheese liquefied white, robbing vivid dairy. Skin clumsily slipping from skull. Bags around eyes melting Rorschach's Skeleton looks back. Eyes wide as grappling hooks. Metallic spider legs twitching for concrete to impale. Jaws open. Slow flame. Billowing more like smoke than fire.
Comes through growing cracks in mirror before vanishing. Skinless nightmare. Blood-thick hallucination. Vapor and memory. Snot target thins. Bog of sink water pushes last of dancing gas. Humidity eliminating shotgun-blast phlegm's brief density. Chrome button in deep end pushed. Swallowing corroded metal flakes. Pale oil-slick foam granted will to congeal into something rich. Lead pipes rumble paneled walls. Orchestral sucking noises. Drain vocalizing wind and brass. Gurgled belch caps off tainted symphony. Vines of sewage followed on way to bedroom. Giving shadow tendrils. Host part octopus. Vines to door. Crawling on wood. Connecting like fingers sliding into open space of hand.

Door wasn't shut all the way. Weight of shadow enough to push door open. Bed anticipating return to womb-cottons. Culling nerves like amputated limbs that twitch with pains of host mutilation.

Plaid comforter. Fabric skin. Crumbled and starched from protein of masturbation. Ejaculate compacting strands into gelled spikes. Naked woman lying on side. Ghost-white cells compose organ. Shrink wrapping skeleton in soul-cold baggage. Hair goes straight down before ends split and feather just above shoulders. Grease black ice. Snow aged by road.

Droplets of sweat down crease in back. Arrowing asshole. Moisture coats sphincter with appetizing glaze. Climb into bed. Rest semi-hard cock in crack of ass. Slowly grinds ass cheeks into cock, massaging sides. Sweat collected in and around ass lubricates cock, allowing it to slip into ass with ease. Cavity chokes with delicacy but with strength enough to suck skin clean. Faint tears. Skin of back ripping in half. Intake/outtake thrust. Split becoming divide. Exposing red meats whose slime freezes in open air. Flip to stomach. Thrusting back. Vacuum attachment throwing up swallow. Up on knees. Pushing back with waist. Making ass ripple.
Grab arms. Pull them behind. Pressing wrists close above small of back. Guts packed with fluids vomited from infected veined sacks.

Go soft inside. Falling out cavity. Turn over to front. Face streaked with white-out and Xeroxed. Long black hairs springing from breast-meat. Spiders inching out of chest cavity through pinholes in skin. Stomach tones. Details outlined with faint hairs like belly of wolf. Set of teeth glowers in vagina. Lips pulled back. Fastened open by hooked wires. Coil around each other starting above naval, running up lycanthropic gut and through cleavage, splitting below throat, going around nape of neck, cords pulled inside by tiny rodents. Abdominal rats take them to vaginal cavity. Jaw wired shut.

Lean over. Sucked in tongue first by wormhole face. Dissolved in stomach acids that broke down fabric of universes ingested before.

- **JM**:

I used to spend much of my time studying the underbelly of the underbelly. there was a lot to satisfy my thirst for the darkness in what was readily available in stores, in libraries, on line, but I always wanted to go deeper than that. hidden clubs. Discredited religions. Cults, sects. My curiosity was ignited through films and literature and when my search for the truth was met with dead ends, my stifled passions would be ventilated through viewings, readings and my own writings and actions of which I would chronicle on my own blog, *Vulnerable Adult*.

There was one group though that I discovered after a snail mail correspondence I had with Richey Walker; the vocalist for one of my favorite underground acts Raincoater. He was ex-communicated from that group after it was discovered that he had sampled a genuine snuff film and looped the sound effect throughout a demo. He was kind enough to send me a copy of this impossible to find recording and we've been swapping stories, tapes, videos and books ever since. As fortune would have it, he was going to be touring the area with his new band Connoisumer and he had gotten a "guest of honor" invite to a party put together by a group known as The Gift Givers; a secret society that worships a monstrous deity known as the Jaundice Monarch.

There's a lot on the internet about this Jaundice Monarch if you know where to look. There isn't any real literature available detailing its history, much of the mythology of this being is piecemeal; a disjointed collage of assumptive fan fiction and they-tell-two-friends hearsay.

The most current attempt at unpacking this *being's* myth and streamlining it into a narrative suitable for mass market consumption is an early 00s video game entitled *the First Worshiped*. The game was pulled off the market after the death of its creator, who committed suicide in front of a gaming convention audience after being asked about the adverse effects the game had on those who played it (hallucinations, paranoia, physical violence in many forms).

The cartridge is a much sought after collector's item, as is the gaming guide that has a detailed walk through of the levels; the text itself a work of barely decipherable cosmic horror.

It is widely believed that the Gift Givers openly despise *the First Worshiped*, and there is even a whispered conspiracy theory that the Gift Givers coaxed the game's creator into killing himself, or that the creator feared their reprisal, thus chose to end his own life rather than face their cruel vengeance. The Givers claim to know the true origin of the Jaundice Monarch, not just that they know, but that they are the only ones that know and only a chosen few are privy to the reality of the being.

Walker was apparently one of those chosen few. I never attempted to goad him into shedding light on this being, though my thoughts became increasingly possessed by its potential. I wanted to earn the right to the information, act like I've been there before.

The tour happened. The show was great. Aevea Within, one of the performers from my days working on the set of porn films, attended, now a big star in the genre. We bonded at work over our love of Walker's previous band, but still I didn't expect her to be at this run down underground metal show. The three of us hung out together.

Her and Walker discussed working together in the near future on a series of porn films. Watching them bounce ideas off one another was almost too much to handle. She went home for the night and the singer laid out the plan for me;

"Okay Helen, here's the skinny; the other guys are gonna take the van. We'll take your car to this spot. We park and then I call a number. Another car will pick us up and take us to the house."

The spot is a dirt parking lot off a narrow unlit stretch of road. He calls the number. We see lights in no long amount of time. n inconspicuous black hybrid pulls into the lot. We get in. The driver is an older woman, attractive but hardened. She says her name is Vivan. She mentions what a fan they all are of Walker's work. In a playful voice she tells us to close our eyes.

We do so. Sitting in a car with my favorite song writer on our way to a house in the woods where a cryptocratic sect performs rituals of worship, surrounding an ancient demon, and all I can think of is how much Vivian reminds me of my childhood babysitter Shoshana and how much I wanted to be fucked by Shoshana. I think back to my favorite dreams of her and imagine acting them out with the driver, wondering if she makes the same noises, says "oh fuck" the same way, and I can feel my legs involuntarily clenching the crotch of my jeans, attempting to mask the saturation. I haven't fucked in forever. I maxed out on porn after working in the industry, but my hard drive was my best friend all through college.

Car stops. She tells us to open our eyes. I wish I could tell you that she looked back at me, took notice of the denim rorschach monsoon, smiled, raised her eyebrows, bit her lip, and we spent the night together, but life isn't a porn film. he's dressed in black and blue, with hair to match. I think about how much I want to make her ass and pussy match the motif, but I get my head out of the fuck-gutter and focus instead on where we're going.

It's a big house. Not a mansion, nothing gaudy or cavernous, just a slightly larger than average suburban home with a wide backyard. There's music playing; Chelsea Wolfe, Zola Jesus, Emily Ruth Rundle, Kayla Takira, Neko Case's darker material, Lana Del Rey. Cranes. Portishead, That's Not Good I'm Not Happy. Sad girls with pretty voices and no small undercurrent of menace.

Vivian brings us upstairs to an attic. There are people sitting in chairs in front of a podium. A design carved into the podium is what I imagine is an approximation of the Jaundice Monarch, as it falls in line with much of the descriptions I've read, though the execution of the design is more confidently rendered. It is believed (among non-Givers) that the Jaundice Monarch is constantly rearranging its own molecules, that it can be any shape it wants, any size it wants, that it has no stable form, existing in some sort of compromise between the states of matter… that it is in fact its own form of matter.

PEACEMEAL: THE ▮FINAL▮ CUT

The common feature in all imaginings (and indeed all the ephemera I am noticing crabbed along the walls, ceiling and floor of the attic) is the yellow skin, hence the "Jaundice" in "Jaundice Monarch". Some erroneously conclude that Robert Chambers' King in Yellow is somehow tied to the Jaundice Monarch, that one influenced the other. The difference is many of the literature and art I am seeing predates Chambers' work by what seems to be a millennium, and there is no one author or artist that can be found as the source producer of the myth. It's closer to the Bible than any work of weird fiction ever produced.

Articulation of the evening's details evade me. What happened in there is for my id to treasure. I have never experienced hermeticism so transcendent. Something so utterly my own. That I live to remember it whenever I want, that my mind retained it so vividly.

Now I know why they are called "Gift Givers".

THE FIRST WORSHIPED:

TYPE: Speculative adventure/survival horror.

OBJECTIVE:
Before anything recorded to document or memory, the universe was at the mercy of the roiling turmoil conceived by the PROTO-MORDIALS; omnipresent beasts of consistently shifting forms. After the final war between them all, only one was left standing: the JAUNDICE MONARCH.

A pioneer at the frontiers of sadism and cruelty, the JAUNDICE MONARCH would openly court to be both followed and feared by the burgeoning species that would be the ancestors of the first wave of mankind. As concepts like sanity and reason became currency, the being's followers dwindled, many choosing oblivion with their chosen master over existence with none. As time wore on, the curators of human history eradicated any corporeal, intellectual, or philosophical trace of the JAUNDICE MONARCH, though many of the being's exploits were recorded in the incidental fictions of what would become known as horror literature. It is the dawn of a new century. While digging through the vast archives of the world's only remaining library ambitious anthropology student/paranormal enthusiast LIZA MONDAY stumbles upon a scroll detailing the rise and fall of the JAUNDICE MONARCH. Compelled to read the bizarre text out loud, she unknowingly awakens the long-slumbering being into this world, sending existence back to the time when the JAUNDICE MONARCH reigned supreme.

The player must assist LIZA through surreal terrains, facing off against PROTO-MORDIAL cultists, deformed beasts of varying size, and eventual the FIRST WORSHIPPED; THE JAUNDICE MONARCH.

LAYOUT:
LIZA must battle her way through 8 levels. The first four levels; The Library, the Park, the Town Square, and City Hall will lead the Portal, where LIZA will travel to the next 4 levels: The Rolling Moulded Flesh Sphere, The Suspended Red Liquid Dome, The Collapsing Stairway of Acid Dust, and finally The Lair of the JAUNDICE MONARCH, which is inside the bowels of the JAUNDICE MONARCH, as the being is its own tower.

SCROLL:
Alternating frequently between side-scrolling, POV, over shoulder, map overviews, more often than not without

warning, as to accurately mirror the discord of the new old world.

PROTAGONIST'S ABILITIES:
Problem solving. Avoidance. Labyrinthine knowledge of forgotten cultures. High threshold for mania. It will help the player greatly to possess these traits themselves or they may succumb to the JAUNDICE MONARCH's over-influence.

LEVEL ONE - *THE LIBRARY*: here is where LIZA must gather the supplies necessary to head out into the now morphing earth. She must find text books possessing the chants that will send the JAUNDICE MONARCH's followers to the NIHIL-PLAINS, where the atmosphere itself will digest their essence. The player will be able to witness their travel to this place and watch the invisible claws of the air simultaneously pull them apart and suck them down. If the player's constitution remains inert through the viewing of this process, they will proceed to the next level.

LEVEL TWO – *THE PARK*:
as the Library is broken down to molecular cinders, LIZA and the player now must fight through the rioting throngs of PROTO-MORDIAL CULTISTS, who are now imbued with the rot-powers of their fallen idols.

The chants will work on the CULTISTS, but LIZA will have to inhale their festering essence if she and the player wish to conquer the boss of the Park; Riot Leader CYRUS NUDESCO.

If LIZA and the player have held their breath for the levels 45 minute duration, they should be able to neutralize CYRUS with one big exhale of the Cultists accumulated essence. This all-absorbing tar fog will pry apart Boss CYRUS's pores and implant atom-smashers into the gaping holes, which should trap CYRUS's form in a stage between liquefaction and vaporization.

LEVEL THREE – *THE TOWN SQUARE*: as the Park dissolves into an upside-down mine-field of belching green lava, LIZA and the player will enter the town square. Here LIZA must stop ILANA CORTIAN, self-professed Womb Vessel for the Reverse Spawning. Using her teeth, she carves in the details of an approximation of the JAUNDICE MONARCH that she had commissioned out of children's bones that have been melted down and poured into a 150 ft high steel mould.

If LIZA and the player were intuitive enough to do so, they would have appropriated CYRUS's Fang Cut Blood Staff after his defeat in the previous level. If they have, ILANA will be easily defeated, as she believes the staff was fashioned by the JAUNDICE MONARCH itself after it dug out its own cuticle from the lacerated torso of the first Dinosaur to eat a Dinosaur, and thus she will attempt to fornicate with the item as she is want to do. This will enable LIZA to enact a chant that will bring down the Graven Monolith, reducing it to an ocean of pulped bone that will drown the last of the PROTO-MORDIAL CULTISTS. **Note:** the player should be reading the chants out-loud themselves or else LIZA herself will choke to death on skeleton water.

LEVEL FOUR – *CITY HALL*:
No boss. LIZA and the player are to wander around the corridors of City Hall, contemplating the existential minutia of their existence, until the Portal to the next four levels decides of its own volition to show up. Once it appears, LIZA and the player will have no choice but to be sucked inside. Here they will be bombarded with a series of images; Seer. Searing name on cattle. Final probe. Pale lights. Red and blue never mixing. An idea of a monster half the size of a city with a cock

that possesses sentience. Night grey shack. Running towards its nicotine beacon. Flash of urban legend from childhood. A house where the each generation was the spawn of ritual incest. Evermore deranged. Barn gate smashed open. Floor drops into ornate pit. Cluttered with large vats.

The monster's semen was filled with eyes. Cloudy flash flood. Cresting into a mossy floor of black vine. Crossing scaffold between the vats, trailing blood that drips into their piping, fusing with the contents. The final generation of boys was so far gone that the ritual of oldest brother impregnating oldest sister had to be reconsidered, with the patriarch taking the place of his heir. The ritual now as corroded as the bloodline.

Legs numb. Collapses in middle of scaffold. Wounds in the arms and gut leak over and through the grating. The semen impregnated all surrounding females of any species. Similar monsters were incubated. Ripped through. Fused with the traits of whatever animal they called mother. They fucked each other, creating bigger, weirder monsters.

The severely deformed brothers proceeded to take turns raping both their sister and their mother-sister. They each became pregnant with the next generation, perhaps the most confused litter yet. All the blood had fallen out of him and dyed the methamphetamine cooking in the vats. The cookers came in from a secret doorway underground, never noticing the ensanguined corpse above them. The meth was a bizarre color, swirling reds and oranges, like blood and semen pressed between sheets of plate glass.

The world was now a rubble of fuck-bloated demons, delaying encasement in their own sprayed scum.

LEVEL FIVE – *THE ROLLING MOLDED FLESH SPHERE*: a sensation akin to that of gargling quicksand. Scraping footwear down to the sole until bare bottoms are exposed to the roasted ground. Tear ducts scoring themselves only to come up dry. One long drip of mucus in the back of your nose that can't be blown out or gulped down.

There used to be women, but the anti-graces that colored your social motions have now careened over into private expulsions of your desire. There's just the red-hot ID foaming radiation pinks, longing reduced to a crude baritone and monosyllabic demonstrations of affection.

Now that you know fucking, the poetry of your adolescence has grown repulsively benign. You just want sick grins and eye-lid slicing glares, which sums up the hunger so succinctly that it reveals the assumption of your virginity's verbose naiveté being acidic in its puerile banality to be uniformly true, that it is the very nadir of sensuality, anathema to desire's real face; that of a rabid dog retaining a conscious that can't help but become sadistic in the ether of its multiplying infections.

Inflated at every muscle. Wearing a dime-store hockey mask coated in layers of dark pink poster paint. Cut out the breathing holes so he could bear his habitually sneering mouth. Each tooth is two-teeth wide. His baritone snarls relate to the sound of snot being sucked to the base of a tongue. He doesn't speak, he hocks.

LEVEL SIX – *THE SUSPENDED RED LIQUID DOME*: crumbling grey urban crosswalk. Dirty snow piled and squared into skyscrapers. Go across. Open warehouse door. Empty golf course inside. Enter bombed out train car. We find places to sleep. Everyone is gone. One into the other. Cancelled sitcoms that become my reality.

Brother stands over my half-sleeping head holding a pistol. I scream at him to do it. She's waiting for a signal from him.

Try to take a piss but a dog becomes hungry at the sight of my cock. Sketches blown alive. Fucked numb. Backstrokes across the scummed floor. Wetting dust. Playacting parenthood.

LEVEL SEVEN – *THE COLLAPSING STARIWAY OF ACID DUST*: millennial pinned to breast. scope slimed in scumhole resin. tamps and pads the blue veins forking at knuckles. willed to a cough undermining the hiss of syndromes. genital amputee hiding in masturbation. whirl-pooling mould rings a three fingered fist. house-broken ash on cradles of infant hands, pocking wood-chip skeletons.

piggy-backing leech nurse. scarab of malignancy. teeth of a wrench down over rib, shaved to a razor bone. held to heart like a sewing needle held to throat. Rim cauliflowered. Sick orange. Floronic rabies blown up guts, camouflaged in sulfur. play-acting Eucharist mashes brown soot between his toes. ate snails off the ground so they could glide over razors without being cut.

Massaging knotted collar, entertain inflicting paralysis. cease to be stock. Body usurped by the ambrosia-void. Rare apprehension no father figure could reproduce without scaring himself. Phantoms and keepers can be forgiven for their plot-hole inconsistencies. there are no such things as imaginary boys. We know it's not your voice, and the laughs between the hacking are the next best thing to a trade of breaths.

N. CASIO POE

Crawlspace frontiers. Dying rabbits like canned laughter. A dead eye's negative grants burning oil audibility. Television static body paint. Horse whipped on a test pattern slab. seized development accommodates cosmetic atrophy. Lines of grown men split SCBAs with horses. Waist high dogpiled human remains burn on what's left of the flags. Callow prurience. Born a witness. Never purgate.

Reading incest fantasies out loud, voluptuous women with skulls for heads eat in aviaries to see which of them brings death. Sand from the corners of eyes, armors, gaps in teeth. Locusts skirting buckets of chlorine, landing in mouths so they can't live off spit. Mould of spirit in cigar-gray rinds. Wreath of nails bent under foot. Abscess like a sleeper cell in the lead stomach of a dead horse.

Pricked lips drained into soft paper cups. Rolling plucked eyes across half-snipped tongue. Envelope folds on a threadbare physique. marvelling like a body at the dawn of the word.

A wirework of hanged women. Delimbed carcass held like a ballet. at 11 I learned you could vomit blood. Calendar girls thrown in a dumpster and set on fire. A pervert mourns beneath a chain-link fence, trash blowing like the ghosts of children who couldn't clear the edge.

Microwave bound hand. Mother's ghost kissed the tumour away. The ruptured insides of third world child brides tremble like guilt ridden rosaries. A congruent siphon. Alignments of stalag angels volunteer holocaustic ascension. Courting the forked bones of perfect beings, masters of the aftermath are black-toothed in cul-de-sacs fornication webbed. gunned down immune network. Black market trial and error. Once knotted veins are now docking.

Wound-profiles clumsily splayed in a flowery thrush. Saliva gunned. Dream of teeth being liquefied and sucked to the back of skull through gums. Heavily creamed in newts, a connubial record of brides with more ammonia than a catheter cult. Saints crafted from vandalized nativity scenes. pulling out their jaundiced wings. Preserved indigestion. muscles rung out over new-born's head. Vertigo tailspin. Ceilings melted over hands. Mice skeletons clumped in the corners of cardboard boxes. Boiling house paint so the rooms breathe. Tankers of battery acid implode on security cams. Ephemeral bondage. Excremental compendium reprimands and annuls banal eros. Meat hook fixtures like the tails animals use to choke their young.

Wall of larvae drops varicose shroud. Hiding goat horns in a rusted coin slot between the slope and the crash. creaks on hind-legs around abortion-matter, blessing the tits tongue hid from. moves to labour pains as if the dance will epitomize.

Surgical gloves littering crabgrass, lobbing the surrounding concrete like the lifeless hands of drowning victims. Girls bandaged head-to-toe, placed upside down in black coffins, and dropped in muddy lake.

Houses built with skies inside to ween electric litters off the plug-in nurses. Staying there while murders are still indoors, forgiving mechanics while pining for analog slashers. Coiling like embryos bracing the wire.

Sibling heads split open, left bleeding overnight. Reclaimed orphan joy mixed with grave dancer's abandon. Razor-facials like a barber shop pole erected before the red could dry. Wired to guillotine keys. Compacted into a vase. Staple shut the cunts that bore them. Disgust muted in the publicity of an open mouth while some part of them is murdered inside, preferably a child.

Cardinal eggs hatch in a child's mouth. Little figures push through the brambles without injurious suspicions... without tearing robes, never reaching scar tissue maturity. A hole was ripped in the bag, toes digging in the dirt trying to halt the drag. Flies drown in the oil of what used to be a face, swirling like the last look of a child who has sucked in all of his organs.

Ebola harem. Trailing the mud from the footprints paced around everyday so they can say they walked with someone. famine victims in the corners of marble eyes.

As sensual as an angel haemorrhaging.

The clay heart gives away, soiling otherwise concrete skin.

Stab wounds blossom when fingertips pollinate. Amputate myself so I can crawl home.

The best nights of my life are all indoors.

Rocking back and forth, arms around invisibles.

Dreaming of the androids that will take your place.

Eyes melt as they sleep, dripping like milk down cheeks, drying into white shadows of body over body, wrists and ankles deep in chest and waist.

Specks of blood like the footprints of pixies dancing naked on the gratings of a slaughterhouse floor.

48 hours urinating in a broken elevator. another foot and we may find legs on which to stand. Laid at the black maw like

charred currency fluttering from fire gutted mansions. Talking naked men down from bell towers cause they're sick of being upstaged.

Leak out of bodies angels tug between plains. pockets between muscles. abandoned voice in ears of brain, scoured from a true terminal. neon-white pinholes outside the vinyl. Tracheotomy manhole. Storm window capillaries. Maul ticket to clouds. Uncovers the watermark like the stain of birth. Cattle aphrodisiac fails to silence the wasp. The sides of their legs kissed with mud. The ribs pried so the lungs can for once feel the air.

Nailed muscles. Crow quills pinned to egg crate face guards. Glory hole guillotines. Genitalia like warped bookends. Stomach acid rising to waist. Sickles gating windpipe. Curdled ambrosia on soldering iron breath. The sutured hands of guinea pigs bleach the veins roping heart.

A room full of severed heads piled into broken TVs. Frozen house pets buried at test site flats mushroom dawns cook into glass. Harikari with a shaft of light. Talking vaguely of art from a cathedral countenance. Tree bark curtains navigate the ichor leech. Selflessness bore the most bitter of conceit.

Born begotten. Soul-decay, serration along the spine of shadow as it hunches over syringe parasols. Rat's eyes crowning stigmata like a bloodworm, inheriting miracle. Umbilical knots held to vinegar drowning pool. Grief rocks in a chest whose hinges don't so much creak as they do casually moan with the naive indifference of cripples throat deep in quicksand. Hexagonal matrix slurping back its clay seeds. Greasing the walls so the shadows slip to one knee. Masturbating the sonograms of a partial birth abortion. Tongue stapled to the roof of mouth. Spade lizard skin with their eyes forming inside out. Contempt accessorized. Ribboned mutilation. Probing for a cavity to die in. A flower bed of abscesses blossoms where tonsil buds have been sewn. Share anorexia. Geode bullet wounds drained from the photo of an eye. vivisection fountain head. A stomach in the glass. Tampered evidence was the first outsider art.

Pressing ear to pond of lye. Survivor's cowardice. Anatomy maps browned from air raids. Crossword rubble of concrete and cellos. Secrete kerosene, rowing in place with scythes, close pinned and rooted to pond scum. Honey comb sponge bath. Entire hives graven on chest. Harpooned to the wall by the crotch of a raging monk, who cuts out two jaws while in the slice. Snot lobbed above head.

She reads "choose death" in all speak – a rapist's waking dream. Breaths like dry ice lapping neck.

Chalk is blown until their dancing really is for me. Hand prints on neck look less like a stranglehold and more like they pressed wet concrete.

The tire-tread of a stretcher that rolled from the back of a burning ambulance. Inverted crosses streak down the corner of eye like the tears of a heretic whose seen heaven for the first time. Shoebox rabbit bracing your shovel blows.

Daisy cutters overrun watermark. Sweating blood thin and acrid as the smoke from a limo wreck. Leaving layers of crimson soot an inch thick and wide reaching as martyrs splayed on iron racks. Untying hairs knotted around fists, trying not to break fingers in the process.

Gag reflex tightrope. Birth as masturbation, spreading from folded lungs. shelved fruit flies. Worms grown nails over heads. Taught to digest in reverse. Wasps lathed in breast milk. A bubbling inner elbow. Time lapse footage of a rotting deer head. Zinc petals catapult beetles with rain.

Dropping clumps of grass and dirt into mouth. Muddy palm prints on thighs, as if dragged from a grave. bruises crossed over each other like a biohazard sign.

Bifurcated by wolves. Auto-erotic rope tricks. Wept in the subconscious, creaky jointed sisters swab fly traps with iodine. Chlorinated IVs. A nursery of harlequin babies. Tanked in disinfectants, leavings from a soap dish fizz in powdered veins. Manure architects oven baked for days in a sulphur field of dead geese. Lake-logged moan of drowned kitten litters. Jangling rat eyes like hurricane wind chimes. suck acid from greasy puddles at feet. Pour hot tar on sleeping head.

Voices come from the blood, touching wounds in the raw. Light boiled all tears away before anyone living was born. Replaced every limb with glass still half sand, anatomy rattled by hardware. Live roaches removed from a woman's tongue.

She hatched the eggs under her lip in the hope that maggots would crawl out instead. Paraphilic infants crucified and eaten by pigs. You deserve to be bullied if their mother is dead.

Soap from the fat of a chemical burned crypto-fascist foaming over elbow like spit bubbles.

Persona as collage. Mythology privatized. a limp wear out your Lazarus nerves. Faces roll forward slow off a bridge of cuts. Crooked escorts approvingly wincing slut identity. Welded to his chair with urine and faeces.

Maggots cake new seams. Forklift crucifixion. Greasy collections of clock gear bleached with lighter fluid. Fingers hook ant farm nostrils like pointy cranes. A spine weight dead lift emboldens cage mass.

Daily torpor in extremis. Dissection recaptures physical peak. Blisters puffed with nitrous. Voodoo doll recall. Canisters of steamed marrow crust the dirt like birthday candles creaming small of arch. Sleeping hungry.

Brain matter eczema. Head full of splatter analysis. Guns cock every time they wink. Yawning hookworm birthing a ribcage. ECT administered in shuffling increments. Ply out teeth. Spinning severed heads knotted at their pulled tongues. Point-of-view vomitorium. Asphyxiate with chin to collar bone. Cooking oiled thumbs press ceramic cold sores. Factory bowels. Relieved of throats. Rope burn crescent moons hooked together and forming a dotted line that makes the sound of handsaws. gushing corked tooth.

Hung thumbs. membrane grating. Cadaver pouch through sewage mane. Kitchen utensil extensions. scalps swing from trees like traffic lights. Teeth replaced with leeches. Incest of pulp novels, keyhole voyeurs mumble till the latex breathes. Scrap nutrients. Fed on back from trash bags suspended by hooks in the ceiling. Rooted from the inside. sucking daughter licks the animals' yellowed skin.

Dog eared jawbones bear a catholic stress.. Tendon marionettes, still birth postures mocking courthouse dolls. Teething ring shrapnel at the root of a winded organ. Trust fall mind crime. The body precipice, arching like a denture.

Endless malaise. Overdose season. Artery hydrants. Rectum deposits crowning veal. Mouth levelled. Ear-splitting steak knife hell. Windshield cob-webbing. Passenger breast feeding eels. Methamphetamine hellfire past cathouse reformatories, cherub head like lanterns on clusters of roving souls. Swan's wings stitched to back. Bookends gnarled spine. Tailbone pitchfork. Pre-trauma braced by armed midwives. cremaster muscle sediment on the floor of Olympic-size septic tanks. Blood tubers hardening while choked by baby teeth on a garrotte, ringed in dust like a warped halo.

Bracing meltdown. Stirring around physical black market. Woman with long straight strawberry blond hair. Pulled to her. Kissing hard. Dragged to a parking lot. Told he had no condoms. Smiled and said "Friday?"

Agreed to do something tonight regardless.

Find her car. Small van. Placed between seats. Blanket over head. Peaks over blanket. Other men and women in similar position. Rows of oral. Squatting. Pushing grey boa constrictor out of vaginal canal. Born with no head. Spinning around a cluttered room. Three colored shadow jumps out of corner onto edge of bed. No sound made.

Capital lesions. Work forces are anchored by a spectre that pools from the premature ectoplasm of hope's mingling coma.

LEVEL EIGHT – *THE JAUNDICE MONARCH*:
Every limb cranes toward the batteries that illuminate their concealment away. What was thought to be a mottled cloak, spray painted yellow as if sleeping through the renovation of the wall on which it leaned, was in fact skin. The organ had adopted its jaundice pallor from a looming illness of bone that became trapped in the being's flesh. The disease's stride to become airborne had caused the skin to slough from its

chattering frame half-an-inch for every year it was confined, a mass of intestines weighing it down, creating in silhouette the impression of a cloak, the back-flesh even pulled over head like a mouldy velvet hood.

The featureless mask dropped as if pushed by the gnawing grubs that formed the face of this being. Orange pus oozed from where eyes might have been. A stream of chewed up worms erupted from its cored mouth following the pop of a burgundy clot that had been blown into a spherical guardrail sealing the being's cut lips. When its elongated skeletal hands cupped to collect the corpse vomit, they became encased in the bile spring, as if they had been dipped in soft concrete and left to dry.

The being's hair, or rather an approximation of it, ringed the sides of its melting head in clumps of thorny vines. A detail one might have missed was surrounding the cap of the being's pointed skull; a series of warped pikes peeking from the under flesh like crown made from the filed bars of a prison cell. A carved crest was just beneath each pike; a crude spiral to nowhere that surrounded the immediate atmosphere with a fog of sulphur.

It wouldn't die before the world it drove here.

The paint on the ceiling swirls. Stars boil. A jagged cone of sky. Lips cup the funnel. Wormhole detritus excreted through an anus in its palm. Scours downward.

Trail branding the circumference of the steep wall. 3rd degree burns are fizzing in a room of contact mics. Bendy straws in a bottle of glass cleaner. Syringe as a diaphragm. Mobiles of shibari. Affirmation is mental ipecac. Every first word in a hard gasp.

PEACEMEAL: THE FINAL CUT

Yellow ray eyes in a vertical pool of man shaped shadows, moving like lanterns that are too heavy to remain steady. Slowly they break out in sores of light, the surrounding black warping into bars of magnet-damaged VHS static.

A massive five-fingered claw pushes through the row of crackling silhouettes. Skeletal, its thrush-stained skin tight on the bones, but never breaking. The finger tips are worm mouths blown up several thousand dimensions, mossy earth being gargled behind dense serrated beaks. The claw reaches up, drawing the shadows off the ground. They slide down the pike-staff fingers like obscure cannibal sex-rites, clumping at weathered-pyramid knuckles to form coal-like rings for each finger.

Bubbling oil slides down the indeterminate length of an oak boned arm, it's melted mass of sick-organ bunched up like a robe's sleeve at the knotted-root elbow. The air that skirts the worm-mouth fingertips smokes upon contact, billowing sulfuric cloud cover. The surrounding grounds crumble as if piled up haphazardly atop a steep mountain. All that remains is the tower of curdled flesh that births as it kills as it births.

No one knows, except that they do.

It is the ancient one to the ancient ones.

The eater of the eaters of worlds.

The good is dismissively blinked out of existence, and all the modes of evil, real or imagined, are little more than a single writhing maggot in the offal of its habitual conquests.

All of Hell...

all of Carcosa...

behind all that is behind all.

Editor's Note: THE FIRST WORHIPPED has been removed from many stores in the country after several incidents involving mass hysteria and extreme violence that were allegedly traced back to usage of the game.

When reached for comment at a convention, the game's designer Rutger Stello answered by putting a gun in his mouth and pulling the trigger behind a banner that showed the game's primary antagonist, the JAUNDICE MONARCH, in silhouette.

BLake ORTho (author of this guide tract) and Magnate Industries (the game's publisher) could not be reached for further commentary.

FUMBLING TOWARD ENSLAVED:

"y'know Sarah McLaughlin contributed a song to the soundtrack of a film about necrophilia."

i used to think that was a good opening line on a bitch. bitches love Sarah McLaughlin. the movie is *Kissed*, starring Molly Parker as the fictional stand in for real-life necrophile Karen Greenlee. closest thing in my DVD collection to a date movie. this was around the time when that "Arms of an Angel" song was in those commercials with the mutilated puppies and eye-bashed kittens. i had a friend who worked in a morgue, and his boss would leave the radio tuned to the easy listening station while they worked on the bodies. he can't listen to "Surfacing" without remembering the corpses of the girls he wanted to fuck.

PEACEMEAL: THE FINAL CUT

i guess Sarah McLaughlin is the perfect music for raping cadavers?

this dude's boss, Dr. Hyrum Nudesco had some issues, but nowhere near as bad as the boss' son Cyrus; an overcommitted Hunter S. Thompson cosplayer who graduated into full-blown mania when he boarded a school bus and severely mutilated the driver in front of a bunch of special needs students, who were so far gone that they played in the driver's wounds until the cops got there. the boss' son was sent to this experimental mental facility, Thacher Memorial... a place that would give Cropsey stress dreams. there was a riot years ago and no one knows who lived or died. it's presumed abandoned, but no one in the area is willing to check it out.

it was around this time that i needed some work. my writing wasn't really grabbing anyone's attention, my band was finding its footing, but was still a long ways away from being anything close to approximating a draw, and i was getting to that age when women were becoming much less tolerant of lacking finances. a collection of B-Movies and an head full of porno moves only go so far.

i got wind of this thing called "the Deep Web"; levels of the internet not found by conventional search engines. mostly it's junk; websites no one bothered to share via links, ghost town message boards, but you eventually find what is commonly referred to as the "Dark Net". it's here that you find illegal pornography, assassins for hire, drugs, weapons, and slaves. not the weak ass club kid BDSM "slaves", like actual trafficked humans sold into captivity.

not having the funds to buy any of these things, i inquired about their production, if there was paperwork involved and if i could be a file clerk for these businesses, or even if they needed a writer to cook up descriptions of their products for catalogs. one of the sites took me up on; a human trafficking site. my job was to look over the photos of the captives, along with weight, measurements, and come up with names and eye-catching detailed descriptions of the subjects.

it was mostly young runaway boys, about 10-12 years old, predominately non-white, which was at odds with the archetypes presented in much of the information available about the subject of human trafficking. usually you hear tales of attractive Eastern European women coming out of a box on a boat and being hurried into strip clubs. these subjects were not beautiful; they had bad skin commonly found on pubescents, greasy hair, they appeared to be sedated in every picture (i guess to keep them calm), they were rail thin, gapemouthed, barely formed humans. you learn that's what the customer wants. that they actually want to read that these boys are non-cognizant to the point of zombification, masked in oozing pimples, frail bodies whose skin is almost always in a cycle of perpetual secretions. the customers probably want to bottle the zit grease and ass sweat, drink it down and use it for lube.

that's the thing that got to me the most; how in the photos these boys appeared to be varnished in cooking oil, that they either were doused with water while wearing their clothes or that they put their clothes back on too fast, soaking them through.

the job got me through the summer, financed some day trips to Tower Records and some fun nights with sexy ladies. it was always such a relief to spend an evening with someone of age, of the opposite sex, after promoting oily boys to sad paedophiles. when school started up again i quit the job and returned focus to my creative aspirations, more inspired, knowledgeable, and invigorated than before.

even got a gig in the video game industry...

WHAT MAKES YOU THINK YOU'RE BETTER THAN EZRA?:

during its heyday, SadeExistance.com got me into a lot of trouble. in the process of cultivating a nihilistic social commentator/ poetic insult comic persona, something a crossblend of Bill Hicks and Agoraphobic Nosebleed, with little splashes of Georges Bataille' s voyeuristic surrealism and Henry Rollins' telling-it-like-it-is bluntness, the on-the rise social media platform sort of acted as a workshop for solidifying this ideal.

i got a fucking excruciating job at a law office near my home. the pay was good and the travel was light, but this job brought out a cascading misanthropy that continues to dwell and sporadically pronounce itself to this very day.

Here though, i was at my worst. I generally detest people my age, but the brand of vitriolic disgust toward the denizens of my home town is unique against others i've encountered in my travels. crude, phony, loud, obnoxious, and demanding that you be as crude, phony, loud, obnoxious as them, lest you wish to be singled out.

i won't bore you with the casually sadistic minutia prevalent in almost any office job. you're either heard it second hand or experienced it first-hand. I'm not particularly interested in relating to anyone; base level commonalities that tell you nothing about what kind of person you're dealing with are not something on which i will further ruminate.

the job was easy. sit in front of computer. open letters. create files for company website. scan letters. throw them out. repeat till shift ends. i would finish the "objective" and then proceed to do the real hard work; pretending i was still busy while secretly writing lyrics and speculating on what would've happened had i known the right way to love Ida Caruthers; the continuing source of my libidinal frustrations.

if the job did one thing, it was gave me a reason to go to bed early. before employment, i would do sleep deprivation experiments. mostly just marathon gore movies, heavy metal videos, and pornography, surveying the effects of their viewings. every now and then, though.. id walk the neighborhood. find houses where the bedroom lights were illuminated, pumping body shadows casting from the window onto me, almost burning my skin and dying it black. this black-on-black Aurora Borealis, these Conjugal Northern Lights were most frequent at the home of Ida. since it was late, and our neighborhood was quiet, she would really let it rip; grunting vulgarities clashing with screamed pleadings to God, squeaking mattress coils fat slaps on ass meat and tit flesh. there was one night where my brother Ezra wasn't home. i found him there, his silhouette retching a cum stain of incidental incest across my cut-nerve face.

there was never a restraining order. Ida just simply erased me from existence. fair trade i suppose.

the job may have hindered my night-time proclivities, but it didn't hinder my creativity. my fuck-slime co-workers served as inspirations for a series of blog entries on my SadeExistance profile, each one increasingly graphic and mean spirited. the job had given me money enough to add more to my music, film, comic, and book collections, and there were all of the same stripe; intense, bizarre, pornographic, violent. these prurient visions coupled with my seething alienating hatred of my co-workers resulted in these verbose explosions that, while amusing to my online friends, who are familiar with, sympathetic toward, understanding of, and sharing in my peculiar sensibilities , could be construed as a warning sign to the uninitiated (which, let's face it, was almost everyone i knew outside of the internet).

somehow, someone at my job found my page, saw the postings, and it was passed around the office. at the end of the day, I was notified that I was to be let go (thought my style was complimented, so there's that).

i walked home, told my parents what had happened, and my naive transparency with regards to my interests and sense of humor had resulted in a brief stay at a rather infamous local mental facility. i had to do this voluntarily as i was of legal age, but i don't know how comfortable i am with the word "voluntarily", as i was threatened with being thrown out of the house and all my collections being sold off if i did not comply with the request.

i spent a week at Thacher Memorial in the minimum security wing, as the doctors could see that the severeness of my mental issues was practically microscopic. i was pretty much free to roam the grounds, even offered help to some of the more dire cases in the facility. someone who stood out the most was a young lady with a compulsive sexual attraction to objects inanimate and unsanitary. there was even some local "celebrities" in the more far-flung areas;

- a serial killer who filmed the torture of his victims and sold them to a much-whispered about snuff film peddler in the area,

- the supposed inspiration for *Headgear;* one of the most controversial "Giallo" films of all time (still need that one for my collection),

- a handful of former "Gift Givers" cult members, and a woman who murdered her twin brother and poured hot tar on her infant sister. i know a guy who sends her letters. he never said if she ever wrote him back.

i was told all this by this wiry little smart ass of a guy who had been my roommate during my stay. despite his tendency to go off on tangents (he was especially attached to the delusion that a pair of "dream demons" were living in his subconscious because he wasn't afraid of them and they were trying to break him), we bonded over an appreciation for sleazy punk rock and weird comic books (both of us seemed to be lapsed super-hero fans, but he was perversely fixated on seeing costumed crime-fighters get killed in horrible ways).

i did my time, learned everything i could about privacy functions, and eventually everything went back to normal. even kept the "MY NAME IS ELMER" tag from work.

soon later i confronted Ida about sex with my brother Ezra, and after i was done throwing up, i wrote my strongest work and suffered a few breakdowns.

i never really got better, i just got better at keeping it to myself.

FRESH ADDENDUM:

soon after EZRA KRUGE and IDA CARUTHERS-KRUGE became true crime cause celebre as "the Roadkill Valentines", EZRA's brother ELMER KRUGE took a stab at achieving similar publicized notoriety, embarking on a knife attack in a greeting card shop while dressed in a purple raincoat, red ski mask, and tear-shaped sunglasses, earning him the nom-de-plume "CRY GUY".

EZRA is currently serving out a sentence of community service around the Star Rose Mall.

CONJUGAL PRESSING OF RELUCTANT APPARITIONS:

there are few things more perpetually infuriating than the nagging paranoia brought on by seemingly universal unacknowledgement. the rooms to which we retreat to tend the wounds left from lacking approval become towering and cavernous, but all our own. long hand became type writers became word processors became personal computers, but the image of its user remains unchanged; hunched with purpose as curled fingers bash out morse code received from the ID. sometimes we document. sometimes we invent. .there is no such thing as "fiction" or "non-fiction". there is only the truth about what has happened and the truth about who we are.

"Writing Creates Realities'

- Peter Sotos

this quote is embossed on a plaque that's been nailed to an office door. the office is occupied by Jameson Wilpraf, the chief editor of Villation Books; the premier producer of marginal literature in the country, and I've just begun my internship.

this was a dream come true for a pervert with delusions of eloquence and a hunger to be an extremist bibliophile, as this particular publisher had sated my addiction to literature that was viscerally severe in its depictions of sex and violence but that also possessed an artful streak of surrealist world building. i wasn't getting it from horror fiction, where even so-called "Splatter Punks" clung to the normative strictures that permeated the mass market drivel they claimed to be railing against. moments presented themselves in True Crime, but the way those books were ground out created a glut of poorly written, miserably researched failed pulp trash whose mollycoddling moralization rendered the power of the acts limp-dick flaccid. Pornography had originated from literature, but the genre had been hijacked by libido-deficient ass bags selling the mediocre fantasies of disgusting suburbanites back to them and by trust fund cunts marketing their pill regiment/period diary as a uniquely-but-universally transcendent coming of age experience. and let's not forget the fucking idiots pumping out "Bizarro Fiction"; Moustache twirling 1/4 men who when you say "Surrealism" think "Ren and Stimpy".

so yeah, a good fucked up book is hard to find, but Villation had the taste and the drive to get them out there. lost works from the original surrealists, detailed filmography's of obscure cinema movements, the most extreme strains of pornography (the word "erotica" was not allowed to be uttered, as it shouldn't be), photography and comics from the Japanese underground, history books that explored all the guts and fucking that school books either only hinted at our ignored entirely, omnibuses of lurid crime and S&M magazines.

there was no pay, but i didn't care. i made some money playing shows (i actively avoid the word "gig") and sweeping up parking lots, as well as writing for some online publishers. i lived at home, so no rent. didn't need a car as i lived right by the train, and was DOA with women, so no dates to lavish with my earnings. i just wanted to be there, soaking in the prurience that laced every book that left this building. research becoming inspiration for my own writing, maybe even snagging some out of print stuff or taking home some of the rejected manuscripts for my own personal library.

that's primarily what i did; sorted the rejected manuscripts. most of them deserved this distinction; a lot of cookie cutter gore porn written by zit creamed dweebs who got their ideas from Mortal Kombat rather than Thomas Ligotti, somewhere approaching a thousand Story of O retreads authored by lame brained needle dicks who haven't seen the inside of a pussy since their own conception, sub-Bukowski poetry anthologies still clinging to the long since festering "Beat" ideals, and swarms upon swarms of ass licking Harlan Ellison / Hunter S. Thompson / William Burroughs / Kurt Vonnegut wannabes. i was happy to mail back these affronts to true subversion with the rejection notice clipped to them.

there was one rejection though that stuck with me. the author's name wasn't on the manuscript and the envelope had been lost. the book was titled *RED VELVET YEAST*. sounded like a recipe book. i started reading it and found that the title was reference to a description of a severed limbs viscera. the book had no real narrative or thesis, it was a *Crack up At The Race Riots* style collection of cut-up fragments, news stories, grim anecdotes, gross out sex, detailed reviews of snuff films... hardly ground-breaking stuff, but composed in such a way that it seemed to be breathing, to be a document rather than an invention.

when i inquired about why this particular book, which not only seemed in line with the mission statement, but almost encapsulated it, was rejected, Wilpraf said something along the lines of

PEACEMEAL: THE FINAL CUT

"Cammbua; the author refused to cooperate during the editorial process, turning from condescendingly pretentious to threateningly aggressive. i mean shit, all i did was suggest that the title be shortened to *Red Yeast*."

several copies still floated around the office like cancer traces; popping up when least expected to remind you that it hasn't been totally eradicated.

today, after each rejection notice i receive from a publisher, i contemplate passing off *RED VELVET YEAST* as my own, but in a way, it almost is my own.

after publishing a dubious "biography" of the arch-criminal terrorist the Guignol, Villation has since shuttered its doors; Wilpraf disappearing to Parts Unknown after being served several lawsuits from other authors claiming that they were criminally defrauded by the publisher.

i have yet to find any information about the book or its anonymous author, even on the farthest down rungs of the fabled "Deep Web". i've never asked about him/her, either because i fear the reprisal or because i want this to remain totally and utterly mine.

RED VELVET YEAST:

A novella by [AUTHOR UNKNOWN]

Some dance pop plays in the background. a rippled shadow bangs on a body in motions of the back beat. pick-wounds like a hole-punch took to clay. wraps loin backside around a fork and presumably chews on it off frame. places a small dog at the viscera of the chopped leg. torso belly down and fucked with bottle and cock after the removed arm cups a damp crotch. A severed head that's been bearded from blood. yellow burns from

Being frozen. the red velvet yeast of the amputations. The way the gashes pull apart after every slice as if being gaped by a phantom. how much it looks like pork and how little that bothers me. i won't even think of this when i hear its music.

ROCKS have displaced the grass, painted green with moss and pocked with greenflies. The rumble of a sludgy bassline echoes in the atmosphere. There is faint screaming and electronic buzzing, similar to a bone saw going through a live wire. The sounds grow louder as the shiny emerald bugs arrive in droves that darken the sky briefly before falling to suckle at the swamp-plants sheathing the stones. The front door of the house opens. The shadow of a young man emerges, beating him to the opening. The flies are drawn to his silhouette. They almost become stuck to it as if it were a strand of wax paper coated in a layer of amber slime. They fall with it, granting it a skin of exoskeletal jade.

When he emerges, the flies dissipate, each carrying a chunk of shadow in their skinny legs. They drop the shredding into the clouds, turning them to balls of ash that forever exist in a state of near-crumble, occasionally flaking to the Earth to remind us that we could be breathing soot at any moment.

PEACEMEAL: THE FINAL CUT

The rocks have been sucked bone dry of their moss, exposing colors of indeterminate origin. He walks barefoot down a chipped cement staircase that winds from the front door around a number of black garbage pails stacked into one another like Russian dolls down to the driver's side of a station wagon with cinder block wheels. He pushes his arm through a crack in the window, reaching for a cherry gas canister. He can't get it through the crack, and as he jerks and

pulls, pink liquid splashes down the window, foreshadowing the canister's eventual eruption as it drenches the windshield and the dash. He drops the canister and pulls his arm out from the slit in the glass. His arm is soaked fingernail to elbow in the almost-clear liquid. With it raised, he walks towards the stone lawn, which is sizzling under the sun, almost smouldering into a bed of coals. He flicks his arm, dropping specks of the liquid across the stones, which soon go up in little flames.

In no time, the entire front yard is a yellow/orange blanket of molecular bonfires, each acting as a thread in a breathing quilt of elemental catharsis. He watches embers flutter up into the air, mapping burn-victim constellations across zero-gravity tundra's of tar lung, holding out a clenched fist so not one finger would be spared.

Much like the greenflies to his shadow, the embers of the rock garden immediately clasped to his arm, forming a gauntlet of hellfire. He opened his palm and shook the embers off his flesh, sending them into the same air polluted by his cast, this time clutching paper seedlings of the host.

His arm was now clean of all muscle and organ, wiped down to a skeletal bore; a crude bundle of tinder sticks perpetually inching toward passive cellular fragmentation.

The head of a St. Bernard is found in the backyard, impaled on a giant novelty pencil. no one knows what happened. There's a mechanical humming and a large burnt-paper brown Pegasus circling the air, wild and lost. there is an open casket filled with the charred skeletal remains of an old woman. Twin tarantulas crawl out from under the casket. He gets up on a chair. He catch a glimpse of one of the spiders up close. It has big blue diamond eyes. he watches it get stabbed in the brain with a broken pool que. It howls a very human howl, vomiting up a pile of wet grey/brown chicken bones before retreating into the shadows.

A small bus, painted like a cloud of mustard gas, pulls up in front of the house. It has broken down, hissing engine billowing like a steam room full of napalm. The door opens, echoing creaky hydraulics. Three blond women, clad in robes that match the sulfuric Honeywell coloring the vehicle, move like music video chanteuses, singing gracefully with the sensuous rotation of their smooth joints. The one in the middle, upper lip sharp and pointed skyward, disrobes, revealing a tattoo of a pacemaker scar running down her sternum.

The other two have found their way to the smoking engine, inhaling and exhaling the fumes, occasionally stopping to hock up chunks of their throats, which hit the black ground and cook like eggs.

PEACEMEAL: THE FINAL CUT

----

the footage was grainy... the camera practically rocking on the tripod.

A young girl is wearing white panties and no shirt , bound at the wrists and ankles with duct tape. She has a plastic bag over her head, extension cord sealing the bag around her neck. A bulky gentlemen enters the frame, wearing a black hood. He stands over the girl. he is holding a large hunting knife. He begins to cut the girl, slicing her all over her body.

Soon the girl's body is little more than a collection of gashes. Another hooded man enters the frame, holding a blowtorch. He stands over her head and begins to run the tiny blue flame over her wounds.

The girl's flesh is now a palette of dark purples and deep browns. The guy with the blow torch lifts her up by her head, and pulls the plastic bag tighter.

The girl at this point is in total shock.

The camera is taken off the tripod and is now hand-held, and we go in closer, getting a look at the girl's face, opaque behind the plastic.

Tape stops.

Cop lights color the pre-dawn with alternating red and blues that never mix.
Cameras are snapping like guns being cocked.
A WOMAN with a camera fills the frame, snapping.

The image changes to a gun in the hand of a young man with an anus tattooed between his thumb and index fingers. The gun rushes up the skirt of an older woman, sloshed in her mutilated vagina.
The image comes back to the camera, which has captured the dead body of the older woman. Her clothes are saturated with blood, spit, and cum. Both eyes are swollen shut by bruise, pus trickling from them like tears. Knives with the handles removed are stuck in each wrist, followed by a trail of wound that runs the length of her forearms.

TWO PARAMEDICS look over the body.

- These knives have no handles.

- Easy way to eliminate fingerprints.

PARAMEDIC TWO opens up a long sheet of plastic, placing at the foot of the woman.

PARAMEDIC ONE helps TWO put her into the translucent sack.

Further down the alley, there is another prone body. Her shirt ripped open, slivers of glass protruding from her cleavage.

Black stockings bind her wrists to her neck like a lace pillory.

PEACEMEAL: THE **FINAL** CUT

Every finger on her left hand is broken, each one snapped forward or back in a pattern. The two paramedics walk over to her, once they finish bagging the older woman. They hover around her, repeating the routine. Before the bag can zipper shut, the young girl's eyes open wide and a scream is let out.

The young girl flails wildly, ripping the bag off of her, clawing at the paramedics.

- It's okay! It's okay! We didn't know! Please relax!

- The younger girl is alive!

The young woman darts past them, her arms still attached to her neck with the lace. It begins to choke her and she falls. A COP runs to her, holding a small knife.

The image turns to another young man's hand, this one with a tattoo of a penis head between the thumb and the index fingers.

Holding a much bigger knife, which is used to cut little slits into the young woman's chest. She is still in the lace pillory.

The man's other hand palms some broken glass, which he places into the slits as she screams.

The images comes back to the cop, who uses the knife to cut the lace pillory from the young woman.

- It's okay. We got you.

- Where...where's my mother?

- I'm so sorry, Mrs. She's gone.

DAUGHTER looks behind OFFICER NICE, seeing an open ambulance. On the gurney in the bag which holds the corpse of her mother. The bag rises, fogged with pink steam from the inside. It peels open, revealing the gore sodden MOTHER, who is spitting out teeth that hang from spittle of sperm.

- She's right there! help her now! Oh god! Oh god!

She looks at her hand with the broken fingers, clutching it with tired agony. Looking back at the ambulance, she sees only the body dead on the gurney. She weeps with a frightening anger rather than a frightened surrender.

SCREAMS that lay folded behind a tongue stapled to the roof of her mouth take shape as they hit the air . Symbols not at all obvious, bringing to mind nothing recognizable to what is essentially a limited intellect. Some are thin; almost like intricately formed smoke rings kissed from occult stencilled lips. Some are so heavy that they can only hang in the air briefly before gravity adheres them to the smooth moon-blue ground. Glossolalia in brail.

She stretches her arms to the sky, palms up. the rain gathers in the creases of her hand like gutters, running in rivers of vein across her body, connecting her to the clouds above.

The water brings out her breasts, highlighting the silver gooseflesh being raised, starting at the edge of her nipples and rippling over her like a 3D graph of a growing shockwave.

PEACEMEAL: THE FINAL CUT

It's as if she were becoming mechanized by the horripilation. She is grinning wildly and bulging her eyes until they segment from the sockets like cartoon blades. She lets out one more guttural-choked scream, which cause her entire body to shatter like glass.

As shards of her cascade on the waking winds of her bellowing, a neighborhood is revealed, as if she were a glass container bottling the whole 'burb. Behind her, a playground is animated with giggling children, pointing and laughing at the store window directly across from them. It was the front of a butcher shop. Rabbits were hanged by their hind legs, skinned and gutted, the necks snapped to the point that the backs of their heads faced the children.

A faint marching can be heard. The children disperse. One of them hides beneath an overturned hospital gurney. blue-green scab on her ankle shaped like the abdomen of a stag beetle.

A mosquito bite grows and pops out until it looks like a tack has been driven into her leg. a spider seems like it is pointing at her, stretching its legs like Plastic Man towards her finger, which is trying to crush it out of existence.

From the side of the street, an army of people dressed in boiler suits and holding cattle guns approach the now desolate playground. They surround the upturned gurney. Face wrapped in a hood of black ace bandage.

She peeks through a hole and see the face of an Asian woman whose lips were frozen in an attempt to separate the right and left halves of her head. It seems living, but is still like a photo. She try to take the hood off, but can't. The only thing she can see is this face. she starts screaming, but the screams are blocked by a ball bearing lodged in the throat. they point their cattle guns directly at the gurney.

Stuck in an orb at the centre of the world reading pulp comic books. The writing is all in prose format, with alternating capital and lower case sentences. The stories come alive as the characters move around, wondering where they are. From the outside, another orb opens its mouth and begins to engulf the first orb. a pink metal tongue emerges from the orb that is eating, licking the circumference of its food.

At the same time they all crouch down, pressing the nozzles of their hoses firmly on the gurney. They never say "fire!" or "now!", they all just pull the trigger at the same time. A fat short hiss. Pink steam rising from the hole, quickly absorbed.

The heads twist while the bodies move ahead. Lina hides in her damp hair, thumbing the cast holding her bones in place.

A papery image of her mother passes across her periphery like a planet colliding into the sun. lifting her swollen face to the ceiling, the pus shoots in yellow webs that lift her off the ground. Her teeth are still dribbling from her mouth on jism spittle, where the lips have now been sliced off, leaving just the gums. Men hand Lina papers. They speak, but all that comes out is dry heaves, though their faces remain in the mode of discourse. Lina leaves.

Outside is the copper of early dawn. The wind of light traffic. Lina stuffs the papers in a nearby sewer grate. She thinks about slowly cutting off every part of her body in front of a busy playground, lobbing the meat at the horrified faces of sugarfueled uterus droppings, making them pay for existing where her potential children never will.

She imagines sewing up her holes and smearing them with peppered butter. She imagines dipping her breasts in modelling glue and caking them with plastic explosives.

She takes comfort in her daydreams of being a severely mutilated ventilation-deficient freakshow. Arms crossed on the bar of a chain link fence. Children with fat red markers doodle on her cast. Cartoon monsters devouring cartoon children. "pop star X rules!" across the paper mâché forearm.
Mock blood shaped like ooze drips from the finger holes. Every child has their turn until there is almost no white on the cast, just one giant crabbed glyphic in near pink and deep red.

The smell of the markers is think enough to have its own smoke that reaches with claws that fish hook Lina's nostrils, leaving red rings that blend rather than crust.

Mother comes out from under Lina's mouth. The pus from her eyes has congealed into a neck brace that fuses her shoulders and chin into a waxy pyramid. Her swollen eyes are in fact new lids, like those seen on some giant mutation of an insect and a woman.

They open, revealing a pair scaled grey orbs with segmented black daggers for pupils. Her lower jaw is now just one giant pair of gums, crusted shut with a 4 inch layer of dried semen. The pus is snaking down the rest of her pulsating wound of a body, holding it in place. Her hair is the same yellow of a cigarette stained VFW hall, its air giving tumours to the sky.

Lina looks down at her cast, which now looks like the meat of a skinned ape's arm. the cartoon monsters and children are raping each other, eating each other, birthing their offspring with every vomit. Their blood, puke, and cum glazes the skinned meat, dripping down the chain links until it's a fence of snotty diamonds. Lina steps through the wall of fuck-gore, which drops like a waterfall, saturating the grounds, now fizzing pink sand.

Lina walks to her mother, who is standing between two hills; one shaped like a puckered asshole, the other shaped like an engorged dickhead. Lina grabs her mother around her ribcage, feeling the pus roll over her. She pulls, ripping Mother in half.
The wounds of the spine spurt green glue. Lina plants her mother's torso face-first into the asshole, which dampens to quicksand, sucking her deep.

She then takes the legs and cracks them all the way open, revealing a hanging bruise of a vagina, serrated hairs like swan quills emerging from rows of ingrown irritation. Lina drives the lower body cunt first into the dickhead, which hardens into a thick stalk of glass that shreds the cunt into bombed-out flaps of skin.

The glassed cock knife now begins to saw up and down, slicing more and more. Over at the asshole, Mother's spine is flailing like a tentacle, gurgling on the jade adhesive its wound continued to spit. The asshole slurps up those drippings as well, as they slip into the dimpled rivets.

On either side of Lina, a crowd is gathering. Lina turns to face the crowd. She outstretches her arms. The crowd runs toward her, splitting when they reach. A row of people walk next to one another, the sunlight at its harshest before they break from their shadows for good. Men. Women. some still wearing their bruises as if emblematic of a secret society. One man stands next to his sister, her left eye covered with a bandage, blood peeking out from the edges like starlight behind a child's hands. He takes out a knife, and drags it over his closed eye, creating a scar above and below the socket, in sympathy, or perhaps tandem, with his sister's loss and rage. A tear drops with the trickle of blood easing its way from the wound. Half of them circle the asshole, the other half circles the dickhead. They all start to kick and stomp, caking each other in the sand of the hills. In their frenzy, they almost pound the mother into purple dust.

But the cut-eye siblings pick up what's left before any further damage can be done. They begin to reconnect the halves of the mother, picking off the blood and pus, which has hardened to such a point that the skin flakes off with it.

They produce rolls of gauze from their pockets and wrap the mother from head to toe in the girded bandage. They return to the crowds, which have dived into the holes they have made of the asshole and the dickhead. Lina walks toward her mother. The girded bandage has sunken into her flesh, creating a new mesh patterned skin with no gender specificities. Her face now has no features, just a blank slate. Soon a small ribcage presses under the flesh of her head. Nipples are dotted at the centre of her eye-sockets. The sternum is pointed in tribute of a nose. A belly button does its best to recreate a mouth. The hair falls off in a clump that becomes a puff of smoke when it hits the ground.

New Mother reaches for Lina's shoulder. Lina helps her up.

Are you still my mother?

Never was. Your mother is dead.

So who are you?
Hector.

Hector? That mean you're a guy?

Not really anything. That's just my name. this is the body I've settled on. May not be perfect, but the other one was very unstable.

Always
was. Ha!

So what's all this then?

Don't know. One of the two who put me together mentioned something about… screaming babies? Nah… that's not it. So yeah,

PEACEMEAL: THE FINAL CUT

I don't know.

Great.

Hey I like your cast. It's red.

Yeah some kids did that. Drew little monsters eating cartoon versions of themselves.

Children are so violent. Not physically, mind you. I mean, they try, but they're essentially ineffectual in that department, due to their stature. It comes out though, in what they draw, what they watch, the games they play. People think it's the culture that influences them, but I think it's the other way around.

Nothing wrong with that. Creation is an act of violence after all. I mean… look at all this.

Yeah. You won't find me condemning violence in society. I mean something horrible just happened to me, but if it didn't happen to me, it would've happened to someone else. Not that it should happen, not that I accept that it happens, I just..

…you just understand.

Exactly.

People often confuse "understanding" with "accepting". It's quite the maddening character flaw.

Right? It's just knowledge. It's the life force of the psyche.

N. CASIO POE

Why do I feel like I am talking to myself?

Cause you are.. sort of. Don't fret, though. Everyone does. Why do you think it's called an "echo chamber"? so few of us are interested in a contrary voice… we bury the ones in ourselves, and we react to those outside of ourselves with vitriol and disgust.

So we're all pretty much the same, eh?

At the heart of it all, Lina… yeah. Outward behaviour is what really sets us apart in the end. I like your name, by the way.

Thanks, Hector. Yours is nice too. Sounds like a He-Man character.

Yours sounds like a porn star from the late 1980s.

Not today, dude. I've had a rough night.

You're right. Sorry Lina.

S'okay. So what do we do, now?

I guess… we look around.

I've always been in love with someone who is not in love with me. I know how disgusted you are because i can see your face suck in when i tell you. but now i just say it so i can remember how wrong i was. The thought of this being reciprocated makes me physically ill. how artless it was. How lacking in self-abuse. How absent of the murders worthy of my desperation. The deception total. The reality

PEACEMEAL: THE FINAL CUT

eviscerating in its mockery. This though will do it justice, cause it to has nowhere to go.

POOLS of snaking mucus belying snail traits glue crusty nostrils to a damp pillowcase. The snot laps at his cheek, connected to the expanding/contracting bubble by a crystallin tether. It's all hers. Glistening and pocked with fever blisters at the corner of her perched mouth. Positioned the pickle jar in front of the window so the rising sun would make it shine, orchestrating a mocking dichotomy with regards to the repulsive contents bobbing in the amber glow of angel honey. All it really did though was further pronounce the objects inside, acting as magnet forcing the putrid to surface.

The window was still caked with blackened paste and shredded newspaper from when a series of articles was glued across the glass, casting lights on the floor and walls that were a gasoline palette of decaying browns and rotten yellows that could only wish to contain the rich vibrancy of fresh animal viscera. The articles detailed the at-the-moment emerging details of both attempted murderer Karigan Stello and the new experimental facility rumoured to be housing him; the Iris

Thacher Memorial Asylum.

"You can't invent them" she would say after absorbing each lurid detail contained within the articles. For her birthday, he found a somewhat impressive copy of Stello's journals on some website and purchased it for her. Still a cheap underground thing, but she loved it. She smiled and exchanged pleasantries most women would express when receiving a stuffed animal or a box of candy.

Silent downpour. The drops are light brown, thick as bullets, and curved like shrimp. The craters that used to be the asshole and the dickhead are now deep ponds of gravy. Lina follows Hector between the large puddles, the rain flowing around them to create a semi-protective dome that keeps them dry. A young man wearing bones juggles the decapitated heads of several house cats. The rain hooks into his shoulders and pulls him down to the clumpy sand, causing him to drop the heads, which sink into the earth. The ground swallows him up to his neck before slicing down on his throat, chopping it off his body with bits of glass.

The stomach just below the surface boils the man's head in acid, than vomits the lime paste that's left, which thins to milk in the storm. Clutching hand veined with thin spool of excrement. Leg bronzed with piss. Cloudy viscera contracting fast enough to hear. A hiss of meat in a pan on a stove of anus. Bloodied by secret police…walks home naked with a giant nail piercing through each testicle. Mocks quilting on a puffer fish body cock. I don't get this.

What's there to get? You just saw it. That's all there is.

Yeah, but I can't apply this to anything that has ever happened to me.

So what? Does that mean it didn't happen?

No… it just means that it means nothing.

Well that's pretty stupid, Lina.

Why is that stupid? How can I understand or feel for anything if I can't relate to it?

Not everything is an experience. Not everything was made to be liked. Not everything is meant to be interpreted and/or incorporated into your own personalized intellectual/emotional lexicon. It's important that we rid ourselves of catharsis. It's slothful and dismissive and serves only to validate the ego of the audience through vague notions of spiritual participation rather than letting the work stand on its own two feet. But how can you hope to win an audience if you don't make them feel like this could happen to them?

Can't all be winners, Lina. Now come on.

BLUE lights from the snow. A throbbing under the flesh behind the ear. The dog lies on her side in front of the window.

Her shoulder and leg erupt cancers like popcorn. "I want to play with it" she says from the corner of the house densest with shadow. She is holding a clump of the dog's cancerous shoulder bulk between her sandy skeleton fingers, sniffing it, tonguing it, drawing back as if she had licked a battery. She squeezes the cancer, which lightly fizzes from tiny holes.

One time he came home and she had the arms of a late-term abortion on her thumbs. She did some old-time dancing and hitchhiker poses, all the while with her thumbs planted in premature viscera at the end of the surprisingly large shockingly red appendages. She had smeared the phrase "Died for OUR sins?" across the bathroom mirror in a mix of spit and baby blood.

She is now on her knees before the dog, grazing the corpse's crotch and sphincter.

Slowly she drives a finger into the dog's rectum, rolling it around, stretching it like an ear lobed freshly gouged. She slides in two more fingers. Tearing can be heard. he then pushes the other hand in there, prying the hole open. A wet ball of excrement emerges quickly as a bubble before popping and hissing, painting the marble tile and smoking blue green gases. The dog is almost split in half, the yellow and pink of her anatomy glistening warm to counterbalance the chilled atmospheric phrasings of the early morning ice. Much of her had eroded away. Parts of her were now corroding into black-grey dust before their eyes. The intestines shrink in the presence of the outer environment, sucking themselves in like a child holding a contemptuous breath in a puffed, sealed mouth.

Wearing the dog's blood and shit on her arms like opera gloves, she stepped over the carcass, now focusing her attention on the cadaver's vagina. She runs her right index finger up and down the pressed slit, gradually cracking it open. she finds the hole, slides her hand all the way in, tightening her grip on the very end of the animals insides.

Methodically as to avoid clumsiness, she pulls the dog's vagina inside out, bringing it from female to male as it hangs from the crotch like a bad copy of a dog's dick. The veins are light blue shocks on the sick peach flesh.

She digs into her pocket, pulling out a butterfly knife. The blade is encrusted with blood from under his fingernails (she frequently attempts to remove them as he slept). She palms the new canine dick with one hand, placing the blade underneath at the base of the mock-shaft. She begins to saw at the dig, tightening her grip and pulling with every motion. She is now holding the dog parts, looking in them as if they were a coin purse made of hamburger. "Do you have a rubber band?" she asks. He happened to have a thick blue one around his wrists.

She notices before he does and goes for it, snapping his finger as she frees it from his hand. Using her thumb and index finger, she forms a knot at the end of the worm, tying it off with the rubber band.

She pretends to slap him with it before throwing it over her shoulder, walking back up the stairs to bed, leaving him clean up their mess. He gathered everything of her that he could and placed her in a bath tub.

Using a mix of scalding hot water, peroxide, vinegar and an eyedropper of battery acid, he let her molder in that mix for days. The stench is making the wallpaper come up in rinds. She put the genitals in a jar of pickle juice, along with one boiled egg and one of the dog's melting eyes.

N. CASIO POE

A wall of human eyes that have been cubed and held together with drain clogs stands across a monolith of excrement.

Its brown shadow is half-vapor, staining the length of its cast.

The cubed eyes well at the corners due to the long hairs tickling them and the vapor of the monolith. Red tears drip to the ground and steam upon the meeting. The brown and red mists curl around each other, swirling, snaking, but never blending together. Lina and Hector become tangled in the valentine chocolate air, swatting it away only to have it stick their arms like the grip of specters.

The vapor goes into the cracks in Lina's cast, making it sweat. It swells and splits, falling off her light deprived hairy appendage, which looks as if it had been under the cast for months. The hairs reach straight into the air, cutting it to nothing, before forming a fine wave that falls into a tornado that wraps around Lina's arm, forming a coarse opera glove of steel wool.

Why do you suppose this happened?

The
rape?
Yeah.

some men rape. Kinda pointless to pontificate further.

Do you think that all men are capable of such a thing?

Yeah, sure. The difference is some know how to control themselves, how to win over their desired partner, and take it from there.

You mean patience?

Yes… precisely. Also some people just can't deal with rejection and they lose it. Others just cut straight ahead to losing it. I think that's what happened, because I never saw these guys before. Pretty sure my mother hadn't either. Maybe someone else didn't give them what they want and they took it out on us.

You think they cared so deeply for this theoretical other, that they couldn't bring themselves to brutalize them?

I guess. Or maybe they're just an asshole and a dickhead.

Ha! Yeah.

I mean… both men and women… ever since we were young we've told that we deserve the person we want, and whomever we want will also want us in the same fashion, but that doesn't happen in reality, and the less adjusted of us can't handle the revelation that society doesn't owe us the sexy rock star or the cinematic angel, because they've been conditioned to believe that everyone gets their everything, and they're the hero and the heroes always win.

People do often bat out of their league.

No baseball references, please.

Sorry sorry.

But yeah, you're right. It's like, there will be this guy. He'll be in his 60s, underemployed, poor dresser, borderline illiterate, intolerant across all the boards, and he'll still expect a 20 year old lingerie model who'll just be so ecstatic that this cantankerous open wound of a man wants her, and surely she'll subjugate her life to his whim, forgoing all the possibilities that lay waiting for walking perfection such as her. Or the obese woman with bad hair and a chicklet smile for whom its Nicolas Sparks super hunks or no-one, who nit-picks every minor flaw and blows them out of proportion, making men feel guilty that they can't live up to an ideal that never really existed.

Yeah, there's that too.

The verbal schizophrenia of the generic waste-oid. You hear these word salads in bad comedies about drug users… the sort of random crime against wittiness perpetrated by social lightweights whose primary source of interaction is similar, if not identical, to their inspirations; Saturday morning cartoons and cereal boxes. Her thumb is encircling the soft spot at the back of the baby head. In the mirror, she watches the red fingernail scrape a clumsy incision. The thumb goes in, tickling the putty skull. As if she just flicked a light switch down, movement stops and the baby is dead weight whose mass and fate are equally laughable.

Prying open the organ port, the cut resembles a maroon tulip with pale insects nestling in the bud. she watches the head get closer and closer in the reflection before they meet, cracking one another in half. Pulling the baby back, she inspects the glass-peppered wound, brushing away the rouge debris.

A triangle of bone drops like a castle door, a worm-thick sliver of grey brain bulging from the gateway like a maggot that's ready to burst. The membrane-pouch comes off like wet glue, sticking to her fingers. she digs out a bit of the brain, creating a tunnel of the head. Using a file, she grooves out a hole large but snug enough to accommodate a log of meat. The brains form the tunnel's pillowy walls.

Opening the bathroom door, she enters the bedroom. He's lying on his back, fully erect. she crawls naked towards his erection, cradling the baby in her right arm. She places a light kiss on the tip of his cock, dribbling a gentle gob of spit onto the hole. Taking it in her mouth, she gags lightly, vomiting thin enough as to coat the cock in a snotty paste rather than a pool of acid.

With his cock still in her mouth, she casually moves the baby under her chin. she looks up towards him, his head rolled back, his eyes shut. She slowly rakes her lips up his cock. With near-seamless ease, the back of the baby's head is hovering millimetres above his cock. As his thrusts his hips, she pushes the baby down. There is a squish that borders on a crunch. She undershot the shallowness of the cranial tunnel, and his cock came out of the baby's eye socket, pushing pupil and lens all the way out until it hung like a greased pearl at the end of a frayed muddy rope. she pushed it down more, flattening the head.

He helped with his phantom-fucking. The head was as flat as it was going to get.

"get up here now" he said.

"Mmmm... yes sir."

She mounted him, pushing his cock as deep as possible into her.

She looked down and saw the fine hairs crowning the baby's cap like crab grass. She bucked and grinded, feeling the nose rub up against her clit, the mouth sucking air from whence it came in some vain attempt to regain sentience. She reached back with both arms, grabbing the baby's legs, lifting them up to her rear end. One of the toes slips into her ass and she no longer knows who or where she is.

They've got what it takes. that's why we're angry. not because it happened. not because it was allowed, but because it was expected. because it's been encouraged. it's what you want out of them.

The abuse. The humiliation.

The same things decried in us.

The same things for which we are loathed.

Because we are without the right muscle. The right bio-architecture. The teeth unyellowed. The cosmetic lack of nature. The inability to be hated despite incalculable flaws. The intentions worn deep under sleeve. Being

PEACEMEAL: THE FINAL CUT

immune to shame. Even we find ourselves deploring your born-a-target weakness rather than their predatory shamelessness, ever increasingly present in a world where their owners hip is disarmingly aware among us all.

CROTCH of fishnet stockings overhead, the legs like long antennas of burned snake skin falling dog-eared across chest.

Tie them tight to the base of cock, trapping the blood, raising the veins till they crack the fleshy tuber. the sperm writhing in urethra like a pregnant eel held to light, all her children sliding up and down from throat to anus.

In the mirror it looks like alien vegetable matter had adhered itself to face, its coarse tendrils choking cock, assuming it was where it breathed.

Confusing ecstasy with the pain only tortures could incite, it continues its crush until the answers come in jets of ejaculate.

ABCESS in the corner of mouth the size of a baby's fist, gestating like an embryo of unknown insect larvae. The dull pat of snapped rubber gloves still coils in ears as a vertigo of reverb. Using now-sheathed thumb and index fingers, presses down and pulls up twice. The pain over-registers to the point of nerve-sheering bliss as enough pus and blood to fill a Dixie cup flops onto hands like the gelatinous corpse of a sea snail.

Blood of which the consistency lies somewhere between syrup and tea flows around mouth, turning at the corner but not before leaving a little pool to drip over teeth and down tongue. The pocket above lip fizzles and cracks in the wake of the drain. Hands are still cradling the gob of pus when moved around to naked backside, where erection is book ended by ass cheeks.

The slimed rubber going around cock, coating it in the pus, glazing sphincter in the process. It feels like flies throwing up on rotten food. Turns around, displaying the shine of boil-varnished erogenous zones, glistening with the phosphoric venom of danger-point blemish. Pulls her ass apart, the white-green trickle of the pus falling in and around the coiled bud of rectal entry like vomit drop tears, presses frosted head to lathed asshole, slowly rocking it into tightly gated cavity.

With every grind, the pus froths between base and taint, bubbling like a mucosa crest. As the fucking gets harder, little spurts of the mint-hued pus shoot across pelvis and belly, recanting the bulk's release. Pulls off a glove, reaches behind her to hook her pinky into the papery gash above lips. Finding the origin prick-hole, gray nail digs out a trench for the finger, elongating the once pinpoint incision. slides bony pinky inside the pocket, rubbing front teeth through a veil-thin curtain of flesh. Blood pops onto the back of hand, stripping down wafer arm like a barber shop pole. waist and backside are crusted together, the pus like paste between wall and wallpaper.

PEACEMEAL: THE FINAL CUT

Cum so hard hocks phlegm with Freudian symbolism, lobbing it across the mouth where pleasure did spawn. scrapes what's left out of the husk, pulling out braids of snotty, tiny gore, roping it tightly around small digit. unsurprised when it dissolves on tongue.

BLINKING like a cursor. The reoccurring tears of packing tape crack long and slow like the fizz of flogger wounds across fatback. Attempts to drown out the ripping with AM radio one hit wonders prove to be for naught. Ejaculate stench lingers like sun-bleached pennies. A genitalia moulders beneath the flannel. Semen is powdered like dry skin on my hands and black-webbed across the floor.

THE OLD woman's head puffs at the viscera, rusted with bruise and infection. The lips and tongue sparkle from the sand as the head is continuously kicked in circles. The cataract bordered eyes are cracked lenses in frozen milk. The hair pinned to the scalp with grease. The teeth once hidden under a dental casing were now exposed as the green grey chickpeas they are; chipped from age and rank with rot. The wrinkles and moles make the face appear to be a Halloween mask reflection of how it believes to appear.

DRIVE a syringe into a bottle of mouth wash that has been pissed in for the last four nights. The plunger goes up, sucking the brown/yellow crude into the hollow of the lined tuber. Staring at fish-eye reflection in the blank TV, the needles hovers at the corner of right eye. Slowly it pierces the lens. A rush of fluid charges toward the hole the needle had torn, swelling the orb to a comical bulge; a pink veined globe dotted with a popping iris. Press the plunger down, flushing the piss into eye, the syringe acting as a surrogate urinary tract. The piss whirls amidst the fluid of eye, sloshing like a yin-yang wave pool. Seemingly on the verge of exploding, draw the plunger back up before literal and figurative blurred assumption could be proven inevitability, sucking the ocular urinary concoction back into the tea-stained syringe. The eye hollowed and collapsed in the socket, powdering the tunnel with pale blue sand, drying the blood like sawdust on puddles of children's vomit. slap a vein near my left inner elbow, raising it the skin. The needle point drips cream tears down arms. Slither the skinny nail into the vein and press the plunger down, mainlining the eyeball piss.

…can feel it inching towards heart like a horsehair worm, gently roping the muscle before sliming down a ventricle to erode the meat from inside-out, impregnating the chambers with organ asbestos…

PINCHING his cheeks and chuckling like Barney the Dinosaur. The coppers of early dawn light the room with Mason jar gold. at the computer, watching a video recording of what appears to be suicide. The top of skull had been cut off. Brain fizzes briefly before drying out. Blood crowns the wound like an oil soaked halo. There are thick red circles around milk fogged eyes. Green teeth gate a parasite tongue. White slime crusts the lips of a quarter-gaping mouth, slowly slouch in the chair until head hits the table, the brain still secure in the half skull.

The walls of the room are the same sick orange of this early morning.

CAN'T feel passion for anything beyond what inspires disgust or rage. There is a world of beauty for those who can afford a room with a view. The rest are walled in with nuclear vapors that have thinned into a benumbing narcotic whose grip has made retarded when faced with more than the sum of pain and fear. All the stories have been told. To break new ground, disavow narratives and get lost in the freedom of nil-logics. To merge it all into a voiceless sensation of random perverse atrocity, caring none for what traumas the events might infer upon the collective frailty of the on-looker, still voluntarily oblivious to their prurient voyeurism. But there is no need for existential pontification. That would be akin to dusting a tar pit with powdered sugar and fully expecting a non-troublesome digestion upon its eating. Here to wallow in grievous outrage while snaking their right hand down their chest to cup their engorged genitals, rocking their knuckles over and under while the eyes well and the teeth clench and the throat grunts and spit, tears, phlegm, and cum erupt in unison, the salts varying little upon ingestion. notice vomit and urine were left out.

Well that's because despite claims to the contrary… this really doesn't sicken stomach, nor does it cause piss to coat pants. It may not turn on or make cry, but it will before it makes piss meet pants or puke enter mouth. Garage goth group straight out of central casting. Swaying with passionless tubular moan of weak microwaves, cannot even bother to disrupt the perfect alignment of their carefully stringed hair through even the mildest of head-bob. As boredom accelerates to the point of delirium, find fingers guiding arms to the bass player's ropy dreadlocks. Pulling and cutting just to see if she is ever really moved. Bees wax butters her scalp. Tufts are matted into circle of insect bites. Locks scuff the floor of the stage like the long turds of sick dogs.

PLUCKED a few lilies from the ground and stuck them in the slit throats of trench babies. Pulled teeth roped around her tits. Opens her mouth. Nerve endings are tangled together, nearly wiring her jaw shut.

Brushes the head of a severed cock over them, mimicking their quiver. ----------------

SEVERANCE connections. The heavy scent of pre-shitting farts. Goes on like this. Attempts at following a thought before it can be had. Rimmed dust yellowed from signature. Rotted molars where the nipples once were. Hiss of coffee milk foam.

Water being chugged from a foot-high bottle, plastic corkscrewed into shape. That coppery odor of unwashed ass mingling with the near-

PEACEMEAL: THE **FINAL** CUT

cold Italian food aroma of recent masturbation.

Hector and Lina are resting on a pile of tree bark they had fashioned into a throne. They lie back and let the blue rain soak them to the bone.

this is nice yeah. Always liked the rain.

Why is that?

No real reason I guess.

Is cause you kinda wish you had drowned?

What the… no. not everything has a goddamn backstory, you know.

I get it… you just like to get wet?

You're sick.

You know me… I like to work… blue.

A pun? We're really doing this?

Yeah, why not?

It's funny how puns start out for us as the height of comedy, then they become cringe worthy, then they become "ironic" and it's okay to laugh at them again.

That's not funny.

Fine okay whatever.

I still wonder if I would be more normal if I did drugs. Of course the one commonality among those who are against drugs or have never done them is the fear of a loss of sense, of reflexes, of reality. But each individual has a psychological environment that is unique to them. That's not to say there is no such thing as a group delusion, but no one experiences anything independent of their own stimuli, and to say that drugs, whose results often depend on the user's physical, mental, and emotional states, only ever have one outcome is almost profound in its illogical lunacy. I see and feel things every day that I know aren't being seen or felt by the person walking next to me on the street, so who's to say that if we did LSD or Meth our experience would be one in the same?

Yeah, but drugs enable people to be who they really are, and for the most part there are only to kinds of people…assholes…

…and dickheads. Hoody hoo golly. If you noticed, I tend to overthink when I'm bored or confused.

So which one are you?

Don't know if I could say "bored", and "confused" implies a desperation to find out what exactly is happening, and I don't have that either.

Could just be the old "thinking out loud" then, huh?

I did start off the words "I wonder", so I suppose so. But are we supposed to be doing something other than walking through white gas and columns of eyeballs?

Like what?

PEACEMEAL: THE FINAL CUT

I dunno… maybe see my childhood self in the reflection on the surface of a pond, smiling and crying while I recant past joys and traumas, arriving at a soul-resurrecting revelation that will embolden what left of my strength, enabling me to carry on into the murk of an uncertain future with a potent blend of steely-eyed realism and semi-cautious optimism?

This isn't that kind of shit.

Webbed rim pressed into clown mouth with lathed fingers. Strain gauge of pencil lead in grey urethra. Shaking and biting. Masturbates in a parked car at four am. Horse tongue lopped by air-gun. Hose feeds helium into delimbed sheep carcass.

Sheared stomach and passed out the cuts to children like cigarettes.

Animal skulls layered in streaked vomit. Flowers like dissected mantis head blown up under microscopes. Pen scribblings that move and produce auditory ambiance. Solid black after covering every inch of skin with swastikas. Wading in marsh. Body stuck in a tape loop at the corner of room. Fire crackers in lidless eye socket. Impaled on broomstick and punched to death. Boat motor at the base of a bundle of chopped cocks. Testicles boiled in red kettle. Lensed cataract. Contacts designed to look like reels of film. Paper cuts in the divots of chapped lips.

----
you're healing nicely.
Thanks.

N. CASIO POE

Aren't you going to say something nice to me?

Hmm… you've been nothing but alright so far.
Yeah. Sorry I'm not more helpful, but I'm sort of new to this whole "spirit guide" deal.

It's alright. I'm enjoying the company. I don't need to really know anything. I had it all together pretty well until this whole mess.

You still do.
How do you figure that one? I'm wandering aimlessly through some acid alliterated cartoon land, talking to a gentle spectre with a torso for a head. Shouldn't I be going on some exploitation film rampage, cutting up men and getting applauded for it?

You really think that's what someone who has it together would do? Think about it… you're calm, collected, looking at it from a number of sides, not letting anybody off the hook, but also not blaming yourself. If more people looked at their problems that way instead of relying on the hatred and blame that only yields results in revenge movies, things would be a lot saner.

… but there would still be insanity…

…true, but there would be a lot less of it. There's always going to be entropy. It's up to those who are on the receiving end of the worst of it to understand that, this way when the calamity broaches our calm waters, we'll be able to pull through.

You mind if we sit down for a second? I need a bit of a breather.

Oh sure of course.

This spot seems nice, right?

Yeah… like an empty beach, only the shore is up in the sky.

Wow yeah… that is lovely.

Sky is aqua green. Clouds foaming in place. Lina and Hector lower themselves to the ground, forming grooves in the earth with their bodies. They curl their toes in the bright gold sand.

They look up at the smooth watery sky. Silver fish peak.

Reading letters that have been written with a quill dipped into asshole spanked after every punctuation until pinked skin sloughs and hooks into fat dragging it from muscle hand smothered in mucous from large bloody nose stands over two glasses pours wine down small of back mixes with blood from cheeks and shit from crack drips into the two glasses stirred than drank Iced dog water oils the foetal grinder with extreme just cause bone is a tumor umbilical chock collar noose hole punched with an anvil in the paper rectum of a cancer hollow dirty muscle car garage where they stage rapes her rape the one who didn't want him well he'll save and she'll love him for it but what they don't know is that it is all real and he doesn't plan on stopping it at all in fact he's gonna take it one step farther and masturbate to the assault he once dreamed of stopping cause he wants to see how

she'll react if she reacts at all if she'll
want it if she'll cum if she'll love him for
this for revealing those depths to her where
weak friends and piss family would shield her
from the blunt embolden her frailty where he
puts her through the paces that will build
character scab her heart cure the mind into
football leather chastity capsule my
cottonmouth grows a rippled clitoris life
support bladders spooled from needle nibbles
the flaking prolapse inhaling the gape
leaving street line yellow stripes encased in
its own lining left hemisphere of skull stored
in her stomach while the swelling in her brain
goes down throw the sheets over the rail pipe
of throat between teabag lungs sucked the
chewed hole bombed out ridged skin a volcano
of white honey foaming from egg beaters turned
on in cunt turned on against ass whipped
muscle in skull top bucket screamed guts in
horse husk troughs

I hate the house when it's like this all the
benign emotional cruelty of an overcast with
the quiet of the day after a parent's funeral
but no body died and there's some crunchy
black noise co-opting your pain as you co-opt
its pain soon will be a normalcy to loath

Lately all that makes me hard is seeing a
woman being eaten out not just tacky girlgirl
stuff but hetero also and I best learned how
not to eat pussy by watching guys in porn poke
the outside of a vagina with the flat-side of
their tongues over and over and call that
cunnilingus but I never took much stock in
having a technique I just sort of wiggle
around curl and puff hum and suck chew lips
with lips see how long before I can blow their

PEACEMEAL: THE FINAL CUT

ass kneeling on the bed Blindfolded Lips slick with saliva mouth waters warm breath raise gooseflesh across form run fingers between breasts glistening heightened eros torturously

snaking panties soaked with pussy juice fingers slip in buck and moan breathy matters knead flesh inside pussy rubbing and patting alternating fast-slow motions battered froth drip down hands.

Screaming cursing grinding teeth licking lips begging for cock finger-fuck harder and faster grabs wrist driving hand deep as possible slip fingers out fingertips have pickled put them between lips kiss over them slurping fuck in tandem bites lips nods take blindfold off crawl on all fours stand at the other end of the room eyes never leave sensual walk on hands and knees ass in air foreshadowing minutes ahead pulls down black silk cock is engorged to the danger point.

Throbbing pre-cum formulating at tip first puts the tip of tongue at the tip of head pulling the pre-cum back in a spidery-thread parts lips wrapping them around cock achingly taking it into mouth inch by inch tongue lapping up and down shaft entire cock has disappeared swishing saliva over cock drenching it in drool slowly pulls back running lips and tongue across shaft briefly stopping at the head to suckle and kiss igniting the concentrated nerves beneath the surface.

Saliva dribbles down from mouth as lips part lacquering cock in spit she voice arousing in its coyness almost erupt across face follows this with hungry demonic grin going

N. CASIO POE

back to suck cock licking it kissing it sucking firmly using hands as an extension of throat nods head mouth fastened to cock explode down throat sucks down every last drop groans on cock pulls back moaning smiling hungrily pull up by arms and pull close kissing deeply throw against wall fondling genitals exchange verbal foreplay between gasps and curses turns back presenting ass and pussy crouch down dive in licking both nibbling and eating slurping the juices both emit lick and kiss up back. wrap one hand around one of breast squeezing it teasing nipple which is erect shivers bucks sticking ass out farther looks over shoulder with sleepy playfulness give smack on ass gasps coos smiles.

Begging for more Spank again moans louder bites lip do it again a few more minutes flip around push up against wall wraps a leg around falling to the bed wrapped on top taking cock in hand guiding it into the heaven of anatomy impale on cock driving it deep face lights up in tandem with throat opening up to release loud moan followed by whimpering coo rides as pulled in by back pushing cock deeper inside mouths, Oh my god barely audible under breath following with loud fuck can feel entire quaking body through cock rattles bones Grabbing by waist flip to back never leaving insides now on top pin to the bed by wrists.

Jack hammering monitoring pleasure in facial contortions. Get up on knees wrap hands under legs pulling pumping on cock grinds teeth raises arms over head pressing against the wall move hands to waist pumping harder moans more guttural groan loudly with one thrust explode along with screaming orgasm pull out

PEACEMEAL: THE FINAL CUT

mouth is on cock sucking off juices moaning on it loudly pull up in need of the oxygen in lungs hands find their way around ass gets on all fours licks two of her fingers slathering asshole spit on hand kneading the drool over hard cock lubing it up coying husk licks the palm following by lobbing some frothy spit onto it. Wraps it around cock jerking it cock is now soaked drool press the head against asshole cock slides into ass rest there while fits it in getting used to it.

It doesn't take very long before pushing on to it grinding it coaxing to push it in deeper steady rhythm slips two fingers into pussy simulating double penetration begins rocking harder pleads to do the same starts moaning with fingers in pussy and cock in ass achieving orgasm convulse from head to toe buries head in pillow clutching at the sheets with free hand.

----

tape bound to wrists fat back crackle when struggling eyes held open covered with glue gun half liquefied frosting cheeks punched for hours 'til bone meets bone 'til skeleton hand slips from flesh of arm loose and low like a wizard sleeve

bowing meats skirt the ground by where they curve speak with the voice of blown out speakers of drunks vomiting into megaphones lobes erupting in pus crusting ear to neck like they grey protoplasm hands and began to choke pregnant woman

legs spread in stirrups

N. CASIO POE

midwife 1 holds bowl of fire

midwife 2 holds bowl of lye births twins first twin thrown in the bowl of fire second in bowl of lye garage filled with glass eyes

----

Sky begins to drool. Big foamy gobs of saliva like water balloons filled with champagne.

As they plop down, they disintegrate all they hit… the buildings… the sand… Hector.

They don't hit me. There isn't even splash back. Big chunks of Hector have melted away. He is a paper monster collaged with air, invisible spaces detailed with wet glue.

Every hit sounds like the keys of a piano gently being tapped. I am soon lying still on a vast mat of white rubber, the sky above me drained into a mirror. There I am in the glass; half sheathed in a bleached wave of flat cotton. A thin tube bubbles from my arm. parts of my face are camouflaged into the pillow. Getting closer and closer.

Body and reflection mash slowly into one another.

We fuse. We wake.

She was brought in yesterday. Veins blotted into splotchy bruises up and down her body as if a road map had been printed on the flesh of a zombie.

Bat-splinters seem carefully placed around the lips of her vagina, like bone fragments arranged for a voodoo ritual. Deep cuts have

PEACEMEAL: THE FINAL CUT

gilled the skin at the top of her breasts. Half of her face is wrapped in bandages, spotted with yellow from the draining welts. Her abscess-lips have deflated to an only slightly-less absurd spider-bite circumference. Her zero-gauge rectum has been packed with gauze that puffs from the slowly shrinking hole in a snotty tuft. Her genitalia looks like the end result of a curved birthing of a malformed set of Siamese triplets.

The level of pain was of such a severity that the senses couldn't register it as such, thus the damage was more than likely misinterpreted by her mind, and caused a complete shutdown. It didn't even know that this level of pain was supposed to kill her.

In the 13th hour, two days turned on themselves. the floor in shambles, its denizens exasperated by blood that had been trickling down his brow. Soon his entire face was caked in blood, three-quarters black from cuts, save the bright-red spots still streaming.

He lifted his shirt and cut his chest in horizontal lines, clutching a paper bag with his other hand. He began kicking her in the chest, yelling at her.

She yelled back, grabbed pieces of 20 glass panes and a dozen five-foot fluorescent tubes. She bashed them over his face. She didn't stop until he slammed her head into a concrete floor. She cracked light bulbs across his eyes. He picked her up and slammed her down across his knee. He threw a sheet of glass ather chest. She was on the floor, the

single still point in a sea of glass. he stood naked in the middle of the floor, a piece of glass in each hand, neck splayed up toward the ceiling.
 kill the sound and turn the lights on.

Give me a broom. I'll clean it up.

A demon skull outstretched its faint bronze horns underneath the hairs of his chest, coarse and glistening in the haze. Each hand palmed the handle of a sledge hammer, the grease and melting lamination not even able to allow the hammer to be released into the air as he sent the blunt metal head of the hammer into the slab, leaving the cement in splinters. Like an overzealous executioner with bad aim, he continued to slam the sledge hammer into the ground, the loud cracks of cement Replaced with thick thuds as the dirt was slammed deeper into the earth. He halted to wipe the sweat from his sun-smeared brow. As he moved his hand over the sweat slicking his skin, his hand slipped on the sweat like a clumsy child on ice skates. His arm pulled itself out of the socket, flinging strings of gore from the gaping black-red wound just beneath his shoulder. The demon skull was being pulled at both sides until the skin on his chest ripped right off the muscle, like a prowrestler tearing his shirt in half for a blood-thirsty crowd.

Bits of barb- wire neglected to pick out of face, natural as birthmarks. A pair of severed arms cradling her as she slept. Pulled them gently off, caressing the hand of the left one just before sending it into

PEACEMEAL: THE FINAL CUT

the wall. bomb rain. Vacant of celebration and historical precedence. It's just arson now. Some kind of outdoor opium den, apparitions in the atmosphere.

Figures emerge from the smoke, the skin of their hands pulled tight by steel wires that stop at their necks. They imitate martyrs and the wires snap, releasing gases and copper venoms from the mechanics of their entrails. Depressing dream pop slinks out of air-raid sirens to counteract the guts with velveteen noise. The repetition breaks the words down to smooth yammering, like a choir moaning nothing. Mannequins topple over the display cases, robbed off glass. They are stripped naked by the music of wind, their dresses slowly dancing in mid-air, as if filled out by bodies. The sentences fall back into place, louder and clearer, and we join each other in weeps of joy. Gain pleasure from normally pleasurable experiences is throwing new light on depression, largely ignored in favor of more obvious symptoms of depression, your presence should be framed when your visitors arrive. low mood, poor concentration, tiredness, brown gown of dead flowers, disturbed appetite and sleep, in its corners where spiders crawl, and a sour centipede slips under your mattress until its time, feelings of guilt, suicidal thoughts. But as of late, I sit staring at my bedroom floor thinking I must be the only fool. it has been recognized as a core symptom of depression, she turns into ashes and the wind sends her crumbling into the setting sun and is also present in schizophrenia and other mental disorders. A mother gains no joy from playing with her baby, I want a standing ovation at my funeral. A teenager is left unmoved by

passing their driving test. mild depression
can be cheered by 'tea and sympathy'. But in
severe depression I am a prisoner in a war
of idiots, it becomes a serious problem. The
'invisible illness' coughing youth from its
bowels.

I am doing fine.

I am feeling well.

I don't even know that he killed himself.
There are people close to him who don't think
that he did... just days before he was found
dead, beware, it simply is not true. Ignored
like the dead pigeon gutted by the cat, used
the media to cement the suicidal, Possible
victim of a homicide made to look like a
suicide through lies and media manipulation.
Up to her elbows in soil she offered him
$50,000 to kill, administered a polygraph
test, apparently passed, With one massive
breath she was drawn within me. Tunnelled
through my mouth, Found dead after friends
say he went for a walk with someone they've
never seen before. Retarded by the morning's
sunlight, Had a U-Haul packed to leave, found
dead locked in the bathroom of her apartment
of an apparent heroin overdose. thought in
terms of beautiful souls. Impossible to
swallow from the head first, had to censor
every word and action in an attempt to contain
ugly anger and jealousy. Don't fuck with her,
The blood pump is an inversion. just bite your
tongue when she does something stupid or
insults you. She has the power to make us a
lot of cash. The model. The laminated gremlin
perched, the wings prideful in their
organics. reduce them to a dead-weight and
cut them off.

PEACEMEAL: THE **FINAL** CUT

The gremlins teeth sweat-out maggot movements with tattoos of diabolism, some grim new design of fuckable bleakness. some kind of whore. Tree-bark syrup on highway litter. dove shrapnel sheets. leather aftermath of dog-breath and shark skins crudely worn past the point of blood-soaked triumph. comforter pulled over body. Cable box blur of black and neon green. shake off crust along the rims of eyelids. The neon green is strained from the black into individual carbon rods.
Last evening's DNA, saliva, and other crime scene fluids have dried.
The bed is stuffed with fish guts and cockroaches. Abdomens bleeding out of the busted seams of the mattress. legs are half in static, rubber with numb wiring crippled and loud. The giants are particularly brainless today, caving in their own faces with thorned medicine balls. Bats erupt from caves of mangled mouths, wings translucent as membrane. suckle at holes in the walls. drum machine backbone of a Nazi funeral, cleaning meat from swastika ribs. raise her above them and march her through the streets until she has completely decomposed. pushed the blade down into her throat, turning the gash into a smile wet with drool.

The sunlight sheds light on hari-kari. The radiator beneath the window is painted with the same pistachio as the wallpaper, the paint's constant exposure to brief periods of hot and cold causing the paint to melt then freeze, making it look as if the radiator was melting. Some bits of the radiator's manufacturing black peaked out from parts where the paint chipped, leaving little green and white flakes all over the floor. The vents hissed and wiggled. The bodies clear themselves. scrape fingers on violins fashioned with strings of human skin. silent film grey, scratches on the negative acting as rain. The earth cuts itself open to accept this youthful carrion. Before the earth can seal itself back up they dog pile on the corpse. The earth widens and deepens it's gullet and accepts all of them into the muddy belly. Every year someone who missed out, overwrought with anxiety and loss tries to dig up the world that left him or her behind. They barely break the halfway mark before cupping their heads in their hands, weeping with apology and prayer. Every year another one joins them, giving birth to eternally crying babies, weeping more out of ritual than grief.

Yank feeding tube from stomach, plastic sputtering light-yellow paste across body, the nerves paralyzed, denying warm splatter of what guts had been forced to ingest. The two-bedroom caves. Flowers gash, dusting pollen in pixie-trace. Condoms of tank-wheel rubber draped over the stronger branches, while twigs snap from DNA-slimed pressure. buds erupting spider-eggs. scalp of staple impaled leeches. Cobblestones coil into snake mountains. The goliath melodies sound fatter on tarantula-leg cords. Organs with shark-tooth keys. Crow caws mainlining two lane blacktop. The bird is rotten, coated in sugar to disguise the sour quills. Reservoir splash-acid.

Vaginal bats flap their uncooked bacon strip wings, carrying flayed foetus in translucent eggshell bellies. Cauterized erogenous zones. A sweet tooth stripped to crude embers, dentures are hooked up to car batteries. A drill-bit of tongue through crescent-moon keyholes. Leeches in aviation black bags profit from atonal mind-crime. The prison bar pin-stripes of sky-scraper shadows look like headstones harvest by the crows.

Grass trimmed to ocean-wide algae.

The fingers open their prints like mouths of fish, creamy guppies forgetful of their lungs. An octopus of jelly spurts out open as vaginal membrane, the violin like a throat. A dog Mutilated and resting astride the curb, its dislocated neck spun 180, kept on the body by a tough patch of skin. It had been separated from the lower half of its body. Split in half, intestines pulverized into the streets, tire-tread making grill indentations on its guts. The light pink tongue was plastered onto the concrete, twisted and crumbled as it hung from the mandible of black-rooted fangs. A little girl walks by with her mother, briefly looks at the dog, then turns in horror, her attentions now to a shirtless man whose pants are heating on the radiator close to the window. paint chips stuck to the soles of feet. Radiator left vertical burns on the front of jeans. Paint melted on them, leaving white polka-dots. fingers get tangled in greasy fibres. Row of birds on power lines. inside of mouth sticky and neglected of chlorine. A smashed toilet, trickling porcelain shard, long strips of fabric from curtains draped and ripped sporadically across tables and chairs. littered with garbage, vomit, broken glass, splintered vials, empty liquor bottles, a severed finger slick with saliva… hard soil cracking sounds as ticks to a scalp. gravel road below the bridge. water filthy, overflowing garbage concrete hieroglyphics;. Oblivious minimalism. Locust wings as loud as a swarm. Dull cream. Thick scent strong, metallic, and shitty. The mice had shit themselves inside out. In corners piles of fur, bone, guts, cheese, and turds; their skins flat and lifeless, skeletons evacuated their bodies through their assholes. The heart, lungs, intestines, toy versions of human innards sprayed everywhere, like a birthday cake post-M-80. a mutilated right hand reeking almond, stepping on gutted mice the gangrene forming from the ripe gash. stuffed wad of cotton. Septic cavern.

Buzzes and crunches a hive of white noise cigarette fell from hand and hit dry leaves, sparking flame. A girl. Dead and hanging. maggots, roaches, and flies engulfed body. Skin light shade of blue. Hair darkened from the leaks above. Rivulets of blood ran down arms from pinholes just above elbows. tongue was bitten in half, roaches praying to it in a little circle on the ground. rope dug into neck, skin formed and cooled around it. pants were half down, panties pulled to side, sticky with urine. Mid-section behind a white t-shirt, coiled gold dragon. above insects and shit with broken neck, purple dusk. Horses entered the field with glue soaked twine strapped to saddles dragging airplane parts and dead rabbits behind them.

Twin bottles of piss are open, fumes dancing from them like genies. Vomit caked boot with strawberry ice cream white.

Delicate white sky, septic tank coming up to ankles dead babies floating in it. two low flying airline jets crash into each other over wheat fields. droplets of beer and urine dripping from hole above head, rolling down part in hair across bridge of nose. filthy shirt, panties pulled to side, vagina heavy

and purple. clitoris tugged vagina inside out. Blood spiralled legs. clay of throat. Centipedes out of mouth, around into ear. raise skin of forehead just before slipping through crack in skull where they can rest within the brain. From stab wounds to enemas. a new shadow to curl up and die comfortably under, not even realizing that their pain is being articulated by someone who never knew it beyond what others have already laid out, automatic forgiveness. some raped boy in her. *Flicker*. Can't stay open. fluid cylinder. naked astride elephant, girth-defying hard-ons with treetrunk-painted-bruise legs that sneeze as they cum and cum as they sneeze....the sticks tap off and the thin metal strings begin a spaghetti western requiem mass. The car stops. Footsteps. Over the shoulder. Flipped onto back. On top now. Dead appendages. Being palmed. Now falling. Left ugly skulls. Copper tongues securely fastened between jowls. back of head is soft, cushion of exposed brain. Two-fourths of a tire-iron. half cord from a telephone around neck. pulled tighter on it every scream. German art-metal in the distance, a gestapo of exotic dancers Hitler-walk before striking a pose right before the chorus kicks in, ripping off their red/black camouflage leotards, swastikas painted over their nipples. Kissing left temple. door splinters, knob hitting crotch. Bloated face of dead girl. an erect cock to nurse into ejaculation, pull back a palm of black centipede sauce. Of chewed tobacco with roach abdomens mashed.
 stocking over face, eyes stay shut. Wrapped in sack with girl.

Beaten half to death. Bayster slathered with bacon grease in hand. Tiny hole toenails made. Girls in black and green skirts....tying up laces. The half-naked twenty-something in skull-polka-dot boxer shorts and a makeshift rainbow ski-mask. Blowing kisses to the elephantine horizon.

Tight hand around back of head. Hair is damp. chest wounds through shirt. Breasts ruptured by magnum. The water blasts open. Telephoned the night before his death, he wasn't always easy to understand He mumbled, working on a story about the attacks, hard evidence showing the towers had been brought down not by the airplanes but by explosives in their foundations. The Goblin Shark has a shovel-like snout, flabby body, and a tail with a weakly developed lower lobe. embarked on a murder spree that horrified the country. "They're gonna make it look like suicide," family says he was not in enough to pain to kill himself. Said he would be 'suicided'. By then, merely a smudged antecedent, unrecognizable as a direct character – present only in angst and isolation. Severed crows' feet. removing details until shadow-black. Razor wire unspooled. facilitate nerve dispensing drugs that do more harm than good. white anvils. Beard black old ash. Grey tarp shakes droplets, needed moisture. Mutual masturbation boxes. The chalky flakes of sun-damaged flesh. The cold sore, almost chromium. scalp a mine-field in bloom, damaged by years a peroxide floods. Voice like a busted vibrator, its insides scarred by battery acid.

Her flesh is a leather brought on by alcohol and bukkake.

Nice ass, though.

a poem entitled "Naked Toddlers Mummified in Saran-Wrap", selfish bastard with a victim fetish, some hateful grotesque. Sand paper drawn back from scrotum. baby is happy. Excessive brightness of eyes. Slip finger under soft spot in back of head. Twitch...shrink and grow. hand over worried mother. runs off. Hands clapping hard. her and son hanging on a clothesline. Awkward man sends homemade greeting cards postmarked from different, seemingly random parts of the country, with crudely drawn pictures of men crawling on the ground, faces in toilets and trash cans, tightness in muscles.

Receiving blowjob from black girl. small of back. Handful of ass. Well-toned. Strong. Springy. A *spank*. A retreating figure with pistol shoved into closet of home. On the roof of a nearby shed, shot through the windshield at twelve-year-old, bullet through neck to base of brain.

"He bothered her for a long time - at least four years".

21... a bright future ahead...dreamt about walking with her sisters. He threw sulphuric acid in her face. Swollen lips seal cavity, granting only a peak at charred denture. skin is red raw... eyelids almost destroyed, face frozen in perpetual shock... hairline burnt back. Her sisters' faces were also burnt by the acid. One guy... looked like a drunkard.... forced them down a dark alley. He then threw acid in their faces.

Fat boy with Samoan features behind a wood link fence. Plays in a backyard with overturned dump trunks and action figure limbs. Shirtless, long black hair becoming an afro in the humidity. Feral, reaches into burlap, pulls out kitten and a head sandwiched between small chubby hands.

Snaps kitten's neck. Thrown behind him. Body smashes into empty rabbit cage. reaches into sack, pulling out kittens. repeats. runs into his house. Comes back out, dragging long terrarium. gathers carcasses and dumps them into terrarium, a full grown python. eats about three before choking to death. Man on a train scratches shaved head with drinking straw.

Charges have been dropped against the man, who spray-painted the
 genitals of three goats orange. girl vomit on a rug. Several people step in vomit, smashing it further into the rug. woke up the next morning and noticed mongoloid lying next to her; drooling, farting, snoring, half erection encased in cum-filled condom. The mongoloid, thinking he was used because she won't return his messages, becomes extremely emotionally attached to her, due to a pathological need for the intimacy no women would ever grant him. The goats agreed to drop the charges in exchange for a donation of £1,000 to the humane society.

A horror movie fanatic spent hours crafting various recreations of their weapons. time and effort went into his creations, clearly a labor of love. his chosen weapon was a glove which had embedded in it a number of knives. A final model featured four curved steel blades that were attached to a welded brass amulet. A considerable amount of work has gone into backing that glove with brass and figuring into the plates curved talons of the sharpness of cut-throat razors. He practiced

PEACEMEAL: THE **FINAL** CUT

slashing curtains before repeatedly slashing his friend as he slept, leaving wounds to his face, neck and hands. He was still wearing his glove when paramedics arrived.

They met in a park before they went back to his flat for a drinking session. The pair consumed around four litres of cider before the victim dozed off after taking a sleeping tablet - only to be slashed as he slept. He awoke to find he was being attacked with a bread knife and clawed glove. He fought him off in a struggle lasting around 10 minutes. At one point he said he was going to kill him. He managed to calm him, who apologized. He was very lucky to be traumatized for life. A stonemason, he told a psychiatrist how he constructed the gloves. He enjoyed how menacing the gloves looked.

He phoned 911 himself, telling the operator he didn't know why he carried out the attack. I almost stabbed him to death. I'm going out of my mind. For some unbeknown reason I attacked him in the chest. I tried to stab his heart. said he *came to be* covered in blood. You were fascinated killing someone. You are obsessed with violence and killing. You are an extremely dangerous man. It is obvious these films influence the way people act. It gives us some concern, and unfortunately we have to pick up the pieces afterwards. The Vandellia cirrhosis is a species that grows only to two inches in length and four to six millimetres wide. It is shaped like an eel and is almost completely transparent. the fish is smooth and slimy, with sharp teeth and backward spines on its gill. The toothpick-sized Vandellia cirrhosis normally burrow into larger fish. The whale Vandelliacirrhosa is a scavenger that only prefers feeding on dead fish. They do not like the sun and tend to bury themselves in the mud underneath logs and rocks. Its modus operandi is simple; find a fish, insert self-inside the gill flap. Spines around its head then pierce the scales, drawing blood while anchoring in place. Then feed on the blood by using the mouth as a slurping apparatus while rasping teeth on its top jaw. then unhook the fins and sink to the bottom to digest its meal. The blood feeding has led to it earning the moniker: the vampire fish of Brazil. The Vandelliacirrhosa is the only vertebrate known to parasitize humans, addicted to the taste and smell of human urine. The Vandelliacirrhosa parasitize humans when they are skinny-dipping while urinating in the water. The Vandellia cirrhosa tastes the urine stream and follows it back, swimming up the urethra and lodging itself in the urinary tract with its spines. The Vandelliacirrhosa gorges itself on the blood and body tissue, its body expanding due to the amount of blood consumed. Once inside, The Vandellia cirrhosa eats away the mucous membranes and tissues until haemorrhage kills it or the host. if caught by the tail, once in the urethra The Vandellia cirrhosa could not be pulled out, because it would spread itself like an umbrella.

Under the direction, staging overtook text. In a fully equipped operating room the actress was put to sleep by a bouquet of roses. soon became known as *"the most assassinated woman in the world,"* subjected to a range of unique tortures. shot with a rifle and with a revolver, scalped, strangled, disembowelled, raped, guillotined, hanged, quartered, burned, cut apart with lancets, cut into

eighty-three pieces by an invisible dagger, stung by a scorpion, poisoned with arsenic, devoured by a puma, strangled by a pearl necklace, eyeballs gouged out, leaving gooey holes in her skull. Two hundred nights in a row, she decomposed on stage, transformed little by little into an abominable corpse. carried away by its own excess, the theatre began to vacillate. its venerable filth which used to cause such shivers, sadism and perversion
played out on that stage…

The theatre was empty. They could never compete with *Buchenwald*. Before war, everyone believed that what happened on stage was purely imaginary; now we know that these things possible. Doctor sexually assaults woman during costume party. Wearing blue tights and head gear. possession of drugs. Sugar-lines attract insects. rain harden portions into sand solid.

The morning sun cooks the insects that huff and chew at the powder, grey from the water and abdominal juice; floss legs and wings, eight-eyes impacted in flatbed molar. Poisons meat with septic-shock richness.
Roof of mouth shredded from the window-sill.

Students in circles, hands positioned autoerotism. Penis where vagina should be. someone taking pictures. girl in rags, tight boots, white shirt, blood-brown hair. wet chocolate a hammer to the scalp produces. neck-ties stitched into cape. Lot fenced off by chrome bars. charred ribs flattened and stretched. Loud tribal drums.. Skin runs together in a bland colorless locomotive. Occasionally screeching unmemorable noise.

Sound checks of time bombs. chamber pot. excrement. The sludges crinkles edge, yellowed from house fire. dragging corpse through stain glass sheets. mobiles of bone. tentacles of innards tangle in a knot of skin. Salt and slug. Syringe fills artery. opiate-skinny nail gangrene. circle of sealed holes. rings of scab. yellow tube unwraps, hitting in wilds. flies around dog carcass in gears, springs, and cogs. combed hair with fingers, black socks hanging over chair. shadow-play on neck. throat sliced open, blood from severed head. fed to crocodiles. the other with a belt, one to death with a rock, battering with an iron bar, raped and killed two small boys. constantly striving for slick institutionalized youth not to be trusted across the street, criminally sophisticated and grossly unsuited for retention. Locket nestled in cleavage. right chamber, the left chamber. Both smiling, smudged with lipstick. seizures. rake limbs. Water damaged wooden legs. After-hours world, red death nightmare. ceiling grey, fluorescent lights, shadows radioactive. Sharks and hounds. Peepholes glowing like laser pointers. dark marble, little white maggots in dirt. tongue with moss growing from skin. teeth. Tongue of carpet. vast mineral bath. misshapen bones shrink-wrapped. moth slain on computer screen. rainbow of tiny ghosts.

Statuesque men and woman are epic against the smouldering ruins, posing for comic book covers. Lizards scatter at their feet, furious at their inability to antagonize. Old paper mâché crust of glue and ink. slept soundly on the memories of children with their heads bashed in, rectums torn and sore from rape. "I was so full of hate that there was no room in me for such feelings as love,

PEACEMEAL: THE **FINAL** CUT

pity, kindness or honor or decency." he said. "my only regret is that I wasn't born dead or not at all." he said. "I look forward to a seat in the electric chair or dance at the end of a rope just like some folks do for their wedding night," he said. He spat on his executioner just before he was hanged. Mausoleum ruins. Baggy pyjama bottoms, light red with little black heart spots all over, homemade tank-top neon orange petite, bronze dull and spotty, open up slot, white envelopes crinkled. Teeth clean-white, right eye covered by delicate wave of strawberry-blonde hair; hair tucked behind ear. Tickle in ear. Fingers removed. Bad haircut, head wound. Found hair dusted around body. Arranged ten empty bottles. Each had finger in it. Pickled. Missing fingers around room, chewed and spat. Empty cigar box, condoms. orange fabric parking lot. massive blood-loss. Walking back from bridge, bird- blank eyes. Fingering obituary in pocket. Cinnamon sticks. black. Shaved concentration camp shape. corpse of a child. Milk spoiled. Soft, warm to the touch. Sealed shut in ebony wax.

Roots dead for random act of violence. Black threads caught in zipper teeth, bullet motion to automatic doors. Marble-tunnel. Hunched over open cadaver, fingers buried. builds spine up, rim of dark-grey hair cut to the skin. sunken into skull. Thin lips.

Pointy nose. Coat is stiff. Rubber gloves. A second-skin, pink with innards of dissected girl. Soft nonchalance. Found hanging below a bridge. Scissors into exposed abdomen. zipper busted. Threads straddled teeth. stripped-mined by mad dentist. Stolen fingers. Evaporated linoleum. note tagged to foot with push-pin. Cigarette bog, remains fluttering crude. unnecessary vulgarities and ignorant accents. yellow plastic. nursing third bottle. Gagging on semen. face first onto windshield. Colorized raindrops in reverse. crystallizing porcelain gore. Blood flows through crack, overflowing veins eat away. suspended by noose. Naked. Slit down from neck to crotch. statuesque as hands pull skin of belly back like wax curtain. Roaches fall from mid-section, something big, soft, and white ripped to shreds. Swan, details in gobs. neck snapped in several spots, wings spread open. Child hooker with dislocated legs. Pillow innards blown out by gun blast. Feathers cake skin, made of tar. Skin an orange peel, coiling on ground. Flat on bed. blood wetting mouth left rings around tips of fingers. Trace of lipstick on filter of cigarette in ashtray.

Logs of ash create pattern on torso. Pink slugs in white ocean. Cut in half. Snail shells. Picture taped to television.
Headshot. copper wound around back of head, forming cone. Smile only gives hint of dentistry beneath. emerald gown to waste. Black and white photos scattered about room, damaged in developing process. Tag our brains. Girl on line for tickets and tried to overhear what movie she was going to go see. She's maybe 19. Low-rider jeans and clunky brown sneakers. She had a tight beige shirt with black horizontal lines running around the back and front, curly black hair going

PEACEMEAL: THE FINAL CUT

down to the small of her back. She had a face like the final girl of a horror movie; thin, slightly up- turned upper lip and big, dark eyes; I was two or three people behind her, so had a difficult time hearing which film she went to see, but luckily those three girls in front of me were with her, so I just asked the bored teenager at the counter to give me tickets to what those girls were going to see. He never did tell me what movie it was, he just ripped the ticket out of the metal slot and passed it to me, acne-grease staining the white. Theatre is crowded. Girl sitting with friends, smiling pleasantly. Two open seats. looked over with a pout and let a half smile creak over face. briefly raised eyebrows pushed lips into teeth. smile more open, letting some off-white pearls peak. Movie starts. throughout most of the picture watch her fumble fingers through a tub of popcorn, briefly holding fistfuls only to let one or two pieces nestle between thin fingers, to be placed in mouth gently. tilt head back in the direction of screen whenever eyes cross. burning invisible holes in skin, beyond viscera, into pulp of shivering soul.

Shape drops in corner of eye. Shadow someone hanged, body in projector. Legs twitch and dance. Arms shake. Neck snaps, head removed body. Audience laughing, boy jumps up from his seat, shouting and pointing. swellings. cuts on knuckles scabbing, flaking bone. blue bolts now grey tubes slurped back into body. Erects lumps across neck and arms. Black cushioning. Wild animal moans which give way wearing black teeth. Thumbing wreckage. Spiky black hair, olive skin, athletic-thin build, fair skin and long brown hair. flashlights to face, inside chest, handicapping.

9-year-old a pink nightgown, clutching purple dolphin, wrapped trash bags knotted at head and feet, covered by mound of leaves. hunched over, knees to floor, wet hair plastered over sides of face. crawling rusty mechanics.

Blood heavy, syrup. pulp- scowl, meat and tubes. Headache enzyme sludge. stick fingers in mud guts and brains. skid marks across sheet of glass. lungs.

Suffocating. skin, bones, rib cage carving. skeleton, ivory mangled in jaw, grinded molars, swallowed rectal transubstantiation. Window streaked with hand prints, dragged across glass, band-aids on knuckles slip off. Cotton cuts yellow, vitamin piss.

Skin closing around dirty pearls - make fist. They crown, cracking scabs. Dawn up close - scurrying away, sun scalding skins. Coal collected ash breath flowing in chipped organs.

Male in tight t-shirt and pants, disgusted, eye open violence unfolding… cigarette stained fingers in crotch of pants.

Locked gazes and smeared blood across lips, cleaned with tongue, cupping over teeth. head on bar. salt flats, see-through coffin. a rotting peach-pit. brush fires. mangled sequence inconsequential. blasts unearth corpses. Amnesiacs. Ass satisfied. inches thick. real noise. nets of cable. Surges through tubing. Sparks. Actions of mouth. Wires. Perky chest in sleeveless top. Body in cavern, iron's slab, dope-sick.

Bite tongue. Girl laughed in face when told she is beautiful, broke boy's nose. Blood bubbles hissed from caved cartilage. Prepare throat, phlegm coating walls. Cocks to left, tattooed in brain, weight of ink loud clap. contortion of wrist. Palm opens teeth. relics boiling. Wrapping around neck. Tugged at shoulder, pillow of arms. Komodo dragons and barb wire. flexing muscles,. crinkled brow. arms start strangling. Ultra-violence. hard-on. eyes and teeth in front of girl. Steroid pipes. Creepy-crawling lurch teases boil. Fist pulverizes fragmented cartilage. Apple-bag. Speciation quench for bone structure splinters. boots pressing into palms, gravity vice. Kicked head knocked back into ground. spattered roses on concrete. bag over head, cinder block, brick smash face, crowning eggs from slits. Curled up coughing, nose smashed into head, pulled from in skull, turning inside out, wrapping arms around neck. shake. snot coming. pulling fingernails out of palms, row of stab wounds like teeth marks from beast.

Wrench in hand, against leg. teeth bared. omnipresent womb. White. row of teeth red. bottom blue. curled up at foot of stairs. wrench hit side. Cut the rib. Fragments, vibration. Spider legs up spine. Whiten flesh above knuckle, skeleton bent

In half, belly around metal. Vomit cough, wet heave digestion. Kneecap chatter, pulled flesh. ocean floor, small children.

Naked, drift, pink fish. Cables crack shafts. Creaks. Scrapes and thumps walls, round feet hammered. Trick ear, heart cables wax. Splattering and drippy. tapped with needles, draining into sewer. Skin unwound from skull. glue-essence. Blisters in palm, Triangle… water brewing, blotches. Volcanic spark, cinder, rock, and atoms.

Cigarette ash up arm. Sprocket holes.

Organ wrapping them. entropy, claw. peels shoulder. Wrinkles fingers, under crumbled skin. Stretches overhead.

arms wrap chest, body pressing into the nape of my neck. vortex shrapnel. wall of nails. suppression tone.

Forehead, coated with sweat. Clammy. Yellow. Sweat slick hair. Bite marks. Fingernail gashes. High-heels. Raised to bruise. Phlegm crusted mouth. tufts of mucus. Vice-grip shadow-drilling tip of knife around eye. cum hardened around arm, protein gel. couch, black leather form. Glass doors smashed. Shards out of callous, glass on body, littered wound, trickle eye, areola, forking nipple, fold above belly. Nail black. crushed in door. fingers across folds, blood flush.

Hand across head, oily yellow hair back. anatomical grease. Pulp flesh around cheeks. lips crinkled pea-soup, stained fang chords. masturbation waft. Shots on face. Nipple clamps, blood push skin around nipples, tomato sauce dumped onto chest, metallic scar across head. cheek tingle when fingering. violently ill for a whole day. bird whistle flicking cigarette, burnt filter on forehead. Flakes orange splinters, disintegrating pores. Blindfold caves where sockets are,. rolling eyes between fingers. wet dough crotch, tied to bed, rope cuts into wrists and ankles, pink irritations. ribcage pried open. Jaw of beast. Organs spewing.

Mother said her family has a history of heart problems and her son often complained of chest pains, but had never been hospitalized or placed on medication.

"I've got a problem," said the full-bearded young hippie. "I'm a cannibal." Two boats are joined together, one on top of the other, with holes cut in them in such a way that only the victim's head, feet, and hands are left outside. The policeman who had just arrested him looked at him incredulously. Had complained of hiccups after a couple of beers. The man reached into his pocket and pulled out a number of small bones. within these boats the man to be punished is placed lying on his back and the boats are then nailed together with iron bolts. When his friend reluctantly obliged, collapsed on the sidewalk and died.

"These aren't chicken bones. They're human fingers." man suffering the hiccups asked a friend to punch him in the chest to try to get rid of them. Food is given and by prodding his eyes he is forced to eat, even against his will.

The case had started two days earlier, when a fisherman saw a human body caught in the reeds of the River, Next they pour a mixture of milk and honey into the wretched man's mouth until he is filled to the point of nausea, smearing his face, feet and arms with the same mixture. When police waded into the river to recover the body, they realized this was no case of drowning. And by turning the coupled boats about, they arrange that his eyes are always

facing the sun. The corpse was clad only in
underpants and it had neither head nor arms.

This is repeated every day, the effect being
that flies, wasps, and bees, attracted by the
sweetness, settle on his face and all such
parts of him as project outside the boats,
and miserably torment and sting him.
The legs had been severed at the knees.

Moreover, as he does inside the closed boats
those things which men are bound of necessity
to do after eating and drinking, the resulting
corruption and putrefaction of the liquid
excrement's give birth to swarms of worms of
different sorts which, penetrating his
clothes, eat away his flesh.

Where the heart should have been there was
an ugly hole in the chest; bathtub. slivers
of glass. gelatin features. sore, chapped,
gangrene. cabinet in pieces, collected in
sink. hinges. Room full of flies, spilling
out hollow chest. In the middle of the night,
shot his companion twice in the head with a
.22 then stabbed him numerous times with a
hunting knife.

He then cut up the body into six parts,
severing the head, then the arms and the
legs. alleged that he cut out the heart and
ate it. Then, dropping a few severed fingers
into his pocket, he threw the parts of the
body into the river and drove off in the dead
man's car, Thus the victim, lying in the
boats, his flesh rotting away in his own
filth, is devoured by worms and dies a
lingering and horrible death, for when the
upper boat is removed, his body is seen to
be all gnawed away, and all about his innards
is found a multitude of these and the like

insects, that grow denser every day. shadows burnt into walls. Rats and roaches, raven bones.

A house fire, slicing with fingernails. gutted rabbit on road. Head lowered, copperhead. black roots at cap of skull, peroxide. Butterflies curl bullwhips, Slice crotch to neck, roaches living in abdomen. sun bakes innards, mutilated by owls. Bowel release. Dime bites and gnaws all over sheep sheered. Guts impacted to horseshoe. Prongs of a pitchfork. Eat turds. Eating each other, inhaling flesh, smiling mouth of marrow. Acid drenched, wearily marionettes with compound fractures.

Footprints. survive on skin, washed with piss chasers. Matted and frazzled dog, eaten on slab peninsulas of rags. raw. Body becoming canine mouth. Vultures. emerald beaks. rock. Fingers around rock, collided with vulture, black tar feathers and clay. Swallow. Hand around neck, beak, snapped, hairless pink. fingernails slit belly, entrails pour. Sand caked meats. Bandages. Yellows cold. thrown up, sand processing vomit.

Talons. Throat. Dug nails into palm, musclenaked, made fist. Extended thumb, cutting crescent. dug into neck, sewing machine. Blue sand. Spotlight, propellers, premature maggots. Copter flies. Tits sag beneath moth-eaten sweater. Bleed out fingers, eyes rejoin chest. pony walking backwards out of her. Shakes purple oils of body off mane. running headfirst into window. Broken glass, curling in womb. pink quills. Sharpen beaks on plastic.

N. CASIO POE

Overweight cross-dressers drunkenly wrestle each other to the ground after they are married, smashing the plastic birds and ceramic gnomes decorating their trailer garden. shove chicken heads down throats. beheaded to punish. wipe tears with dishrags. deer head. rhino-horn in eye socket. huffing wig, urine condensation. knife fight. Cotton. Clouds. Slaves trade vignettes not realizing the very same thing is on the television. Now they are arguing over who must walk in whose shadows. They will just merge into monstrous Rorschach, more rich with ink then they could possibly imagine. In their excitement they slit everyone's bellies with their raven-black talons. They're buried in a gash of earth alongside the dead and wounded. Someone will give birth to them again. I pulled the cat from the fire and cradled it just before it crumbled in my arms.

Orange sparks quickly cool into black flakes of soot on my forearms. The rubble still pops, showing off the new minutes of its youth, still warm with flame. Paraplegic. Cannibalism. eviscerate. Farting ass. tattered cat at piano keys. Apple seeds. Spiders. salival-slick. Hair aggravates gagreflex...crab-grass, dead wheat. Rape. crowbar swallowed.

Streaks on windows next to tongue. yellowed paper in cranial ash tray. pulp infest. pavement. brain stem. wings pull skin. nest. Fellatio, mouthful of broken glass. veil. sludge peeled worms. Circled ditch for 36 hours. cuts out eyes. canine and molars. bullet chew. Calm.

Dirty pink houses, crotch of rape victim in dirt, strangled with bracelets, halting blood until bruises chilly wounds. Smell scalp, scabby from bleaching. slow-burn figures. Curl up, head buried in chest, eyes, cheeks. ass-meat, chainsaw, bones in music. hourglass, aura rising. Steam from garbage can. mute voice numb lips. Waving pale hand, nicotine shouts. angel's heart flat-lining; tumbles over phlegm, gravel grinding.

Cock throbbing, ejaculate rape, violated cavity, acid. sweat tasting glaze. copulation-crime-wound-poetry.

Holes, stenciled gashes, twitching blades, crushing brain in vice. Empty lungs, dryheave neck, ear to lips, rack body with mutilation. cut off fingers. stitched back dislocated, displaying teeth marks. crotch hollowed, back of ass stuffed vinegar-soaked cleaned teeth, peeking from mask, drawstring tightened, extension cord.

Tied at ankles, no bones. lurches sputters yelping. days as mouth and cunt of teenager, raped clay of organs.

Back alley wet with yellow. streetlights. pride of rapist. face, void, arousal, jail clenched-teeth. Cage. tears. Stomach to floor, breasts flattened. Waved sweat soaked flesh . Stabs waist. Blood, saliva, semen, salts flung. cry muffled by hand. Hand grabbed throat. pulled upwards. ridges of spine snap. Punch in rib cage. Hands grabbed hair, scream. Lava aesthetics. Black ash. Shake, separate and corrode. Sets of lungs. restroom. legs numb, lethargy, marble. serpents. tingle entropy, toilet paper, crinkled and stuck to porcelain. Exploding flooding pulling grips. floating bloated bodies velvet tongues. bruise- dominance.

cement caking. exploding rings of light. mouthwash. Chugged down. Melt esophagus. Shrapnel. Swish cement mixer, germ incinerate. Mixed foam. Faucet thins whitelight bubbles. Piss rivulets of the sewers. teeth green. Inside of mouth blistered. needle into left breast... translucent crescent nipple. face popped...melted...scalp marked with children's bloody foot prints.

Pulled needle, placed thumb and index around blister, squeezed the brown water out pinholes. Belligerent anatomy. ruptured capillaries, greasy mangled hair. Mud sharks gutted, innards rung out over a radiator. Children palm bullets, mongoloid creases. child biting down on arm. blisters from hot plate. children with teeth pulled out of head, toothless grin chewing at eye.
 red brain. venom-heavy arms putting strain on wire. wounds dripping with toxins. White bandages. thistles protrude. wooden chair sinks in sand. doll slippers in the assgroove. clenches jaw. Pills from mouth. static face frosted, dried up seeds, urinedamaged. children's lesions.

Slip tumor. His brother's child runs from assembly line fire arms with that first hit of Extasy or Ex or E, the further the abbreviation the more potent the dose. I could see him, caked in unknown blood and clad in loose-fitting briefs, hair a mangled quaff, his tattoos he received in training a memory to break all hearts, screaming on the shoulder of an empty highway against the black of three o'clock in the morning soon to be at the maniacal mouth of an asylum or skull to the blunt end of a cop's more defined third arm.

PEACEMEAL: THE FINAL CUT

His mother's father in law, over 80 years of mouth and genitalia reduced to useless mounds of clay. He doesn't sleep, he just awaits to be awake. Commode fields. blackout tits. hammocks of netted hamburger. gush menstruation. Virgin wishbones. black mass gassing brains with paint fumes. Skull caps form into asses. Rape propels. Crumbled paper. girl's tongue. berate prayer. gasoline splashes. hair goes up, kerosene straw. cardiac with shrieks. girl molested, cock hammering orifice. naked and bald, curled up pale against black dirt. camera, confetti. corpse of girl, Rorschach of mud. Strung up. dragging corpse. torn, drawn and quartered.

Vagina fat with bruise.

Eraser shavings slivered lead brushed. Puddles of sludge, combs frizzed hair with wire. warped clay. bristles impale ticks, scalp. antennas, crooked spines. belching heart-shaped mouths, boot grids. Wound unison. Pipe bombs. filters of the septic tank. sewage, vomiting syrup. Diarrhea oily. Mosquitoes surface. Factories detailing faces with salt water. Eviscerate. zebraskin chant sheets. maroon gowns.. Orgasm, piano wire marrow singes. genitals moist with masturbation, fingerprints warped from saliva and come. legs broken. blades swaying. bitten crab. bloated drowning victims. eyes vacuum chrome spotlights. halo of vultures. jaws in-lined with bricks.

Skin slips above and over elbow, salivating. cattle stillborn. Cock-tickler tonsils in chlorine. iron lungs.
 cleaning solvent. body cast. mirror cloudy with masturbation. Creased flesh frayed denim, deforming...public hanging, Crinkled

fist, brick dark pink clay molded by action figure parts. cables eat vultures.

Needles. thistles, chromed wetness. spoilage mouth atrophy.

He gently pats the blood from the welt in his forehead with a white tissue, dampened into a soft red. He pulls the mirror back and rifles through its insides. He grabs a bandage, sticks it tight against the wound, the flesh-colored wax now fashioned with a tiny crimson spark at its center. The bandage moves with every crinkle of his brow.

The doorway led back into the bedroom. A woman sleeps on her side, sculpted beneath the comforter. He sits at the foot of the bed, his back to her, pulls his shirt over his head to display the lion-like dagger formations on his back. Long fingernail- cuts. The woman creeks her eyes open, their veined cream bubbling from the slits.

She gets on her knees, crawls towards the claw marks on his back. She slinks the rubyfat of tongue from her jaw and places its tip at the base of one of the claw marks. Slowly she licks upward, savoring the metallic particles of the Eros-puncture wounds.

Her tongue made its way around his neck, leaving a thick salival
 trace, like a slug made of human skin. She follows it to his face, unhinging her legs and pressing her waist against his.

With her teeth, gleaming with the seduction of fangs, she slowly peels the bandage off, spitting it across the room, then immediately open-mouth kissed the wound, inhaling and exhaling over it with reptilian intensity.

Her legs and arms tighten around his back in a python vice-grip, pushing his blood up to the wound, where she sucked out the plasma and replaced it with her own salts.

------- vomiting. evisceration pink meat and grey brains viscera. chains dog hearts husk of torso

----

We kiss, passing the spider eggs from one mouth to the other, back and forth.

This game we play, see what happens first; the eggs hatching or getting swallowed or gagging or vomiting or some blend of the above. Sometimes they get mashed in our teeth as we playfully try to chew on each other's tongues. I think we swallowed an equal amount.

Then we fuck.

She's on top of me, her waist moving counter-current to mine, sweat plastering her white t-shirt tight to her body, like a second salty skin. I catch a glimpse of her ass in the mirror, my balls appearing and disappearing, purple and pained from the storage of ejaculate that I hold back, trying to come with her, after her, or at least not too soon. Mercifully, I come, feeling my cock drown in the condom, submerged in DNA at the same time as her (or at the same time she pretends too). She rolls her eyes back a little, jerks her pale limbs just enough to not give off the impression of being completely full of shit, then starts to cough out grunts and moans, little drops of saliva coming out of her mouth like a spider-web a child walked through.

Her coughing gets more hoarse.

Twin spiders crawl out of her mouth on the twelfth cough, six more on the thirteenth.

Suddenly the coughing just stopped and she kept her mouth open, letting all the spiders crawl out of her cranial cavities.

Bigger ones, tarantulas and brown recluses, came out of her crotch, which floated an inch over me. They fell to my crotch then quickly scurried off, the thistles of their abdomens and legs leaving rug-burn streaks.

The spiders had completely covered her skin, leaving only her long dirty red hair exposed. I ran my fingers through the grease and tangle before clearing some of the spiders from her face.

She had been bitten, her entire face swollen into little purple hills, some with green overtones. Little chromium craters topped them off, dripping with venom. The rest of the spiders fall off her body, dead, their fangs broken off into her skin, the poisons now streaking her veins with infection.

The surviving arachnids carry their dead into the radiator, followed by the rest of them, marching into the vents, dark purple smoke now billowing from them. The old-coal smell of burnt spider-carcasses still lingers in the air. The smoke painted the ceiling fragment just above the radiator with all the colors of a third-degree burn rainbow.

PEACEMEAL: THE **FINAL** CUT

----

philosophy-laden and often violent pornography done while in prison, living scandalous and repeatedly abused, which he had heard was an aphrodisiac. his skull was later removed from the grave, an unprecedented examination of the peculiar motivations, an uncanny understanding of myriad aspects of pornography involving children. found in the apartment of grave robbers, his ability to rape a blank page, the proper forum for angry poetry and rants.

Life in society, civic-minded thrill-seeking utter bore. institute complete automation. biological accident, incomplete set of chromosomes, be deficient, emotionally limited. the family, the tribe, not the individual. aborted at the gene stage. The authors are hypocrites, their thoughts aborted too late, producing retards and the bait of dumpster diving. It's easy to hate with a cock, ignorant of its fit into the cunt, is plowing it's heavily salted soup into the sandpaper and hallway of the "frigid". how to get dry again, the remembrance for his dagger as I kissed the baby brother as I walked. founded the sexual orientation concealed, the daughter of a distinguished minister, discharged for psychological reasons, a budding erotic attachment failing to report a murder. forging narcotics prescription which could supposedly ease opiate addiction, printing plates smuggled across borders, Legs, Hips, and Behind in Pink Silks of a Dirty Old Man. a girl was raped by sperm and eggs combined with domineering personality and inferior vehicle, chronic life, intense physical depression-battled stomach pain. preparing body, cheap glue. claw hammers. abortions smashing bodies. slit bellies wide open. sawdust and millipedes. cicada-drone, pretty heads. chemical- sludge. Locked in small space, flushing junk, soggy pulp out of mouth. chuck of human heart.

Warm. Wet. lips of girl. Wreckage. uncollected garbage blockades, cottonslicks. frostbite blush. opening mouths.

paints rags.. thorn. venom...chlorophyll....formaldehyde. Pig's blood...cow urine...birth canal bath water.... emoting napalm... lips trace mustard gas. imprint. creases of curb... sheer hell smoke. split streets...melting tar...swabs. gaping.

The sky looks like dog meat. Hairless, cleaned canine flesh, clouds leaving thick black branding scratches.

It rained bats last night, white and grey ones. Their wings are all twisted, like snapped wishbones in rubber sheets. Hanged children are inside out, the fruit of dead trees. The vultures are sick this morning, nauseous from the spoiled underdeveloped child meat.

The street wets its concrete tongue. The houses are painted with loud television static. The doors break themselves down to display the throats of the homesteads, soaking the dry air with the humid urine breathes of toothless mouths.

PEACEMEAL: THE **FINAL** CUT

The atmosphere digs its thin claws into my nostrils, fingering the mucus before reaching down my throat, I can feel it clenching its grip on my heart. The particles are strangled out of me as I become part of the noxious aura of the world.

Half of her skin is water, eels moving around inside her, rippling the delicate cream into vanilla waves. Dragon flies dip their tails into her as they fornicate. Some dare to call her anything but an ocean, an aquatic heavenly body. I know better.

I know sharks are under there as well, waiting to pick up on the meat staring down their kingdom.

The particles have collected back into the pathetic mass that is I. The apparitions that carried me relax their limbs to drop me to the earth, where I have been all along.

I wake up on this flat-bed of earthly asphalt, sweating sour dew. I'm blanketed by a patchwork cloth of leaves, some tattooed with boot prints. A blackened pile of rocks and twigs is still smoldering across from me. Twin trail of urine form into an X on top of the charred nature, this effigy minus a body, save for some rats and one gutted possum, as if the birds of prey were trying to burn the evidence.

There's a maul ticket in my hand. Some girl dropped them on us last night, good for one free wolf-jaw to the neck. Some think they'll turn into werewolves after these encounters. Those with a lyco-fetish may be inclined to purchase a maul-ticket for their boyfriend or girlfriend.

N. CASIO POE

A slightly defined silhouette is blacking out the vomit-emerald sky. Some of his flesh drips onto my face, gooey and warm like pizza cheese. His dislocated his own arm pulling me up, pointing to the lake. Skin floated as a fluid on the lake, thin like oil, little veins of red tracked over the elixir. His intestines were now melted plastic or wet dough falling to the ground, tightly coiled into a pile before joining the soup that was his flesh.

The wind knocked over his skeleton, smashed into dust by the dirt and air.

The sun blackened the leafless trees into veined shadows. Single rows of trees lined up on both sides of the road, creating a roofless jagged tunnel over the empty highway. The brown trunks grew out of the piles of snow, which were aging into dirtstained crumbling glaciers. A flock of birds flew over my head.

They were disemboweled, guts and feathers plucked, plummeting and flaking down (respectively). The ones left uncut carried a man, his face scarred by talons and beaks. His mid-section had one vertical cut that acted as an arrow pointing to his mutilated crotch. The birds turned his back to me, his spine exposed. Using their beaks they pried open his rib cage until both halves faced me. They spun him around until we were face to face again. They never stopped flying. The man's innards fell, intestine rolling out of his body like the rope ladder of a helicopter. It smacked me in the face and wrapped itself around me like a faceless albino python, pulling me into the air. My feet feel a slight tingle as they graze the power lines. I feel a much more substantial pain when my stomach plows into a streetlight, causing the organic noose to finally snap, dropping me into a pond of wet cement just in front of a big house. I observe my imprint in the cement. The intestine made it look as if I had a tail.

I turn to the house in front of me, in sync with the thunder claps and darkening skies. It begins to rain. The bottom of each step collected the rain like cement gutters.

Lightning sporadically outlined the ashclouds. My feet are bare, soaked in the heavy rain water that seems to seep through the callous.
The house seems a thousand feet tall, as overbearing as the gates of Hell. I only have to walk a few inches, as the house follows them and we meet.

The doorbell sounds like a slashing knife. The doorway releases a cold refrigerator light, a figure fading into definition at its center. The woman is clad in a skinny black t-shirt and crimson panties. Her hair is icy black, straddling that fine line between shiny and greasy. It stops just below her pillowy lips. She's almost as pale a crystal as the light surrounding her.

There's a gun to my head. The handle is in my right hand. I smile with an open mouth, hoping she can catch the blast. She watches the bullet pass behind my eyes and crash through my left temple, brain segments, blood streams, and bone splinters spraying in any and all directions.

Just before I hit the ground I come back up in a rewind motion.

I glare straight through her. My head is hollowed out from the blast, a bulk of dark red and pink on the ground being washed clean by the rain. The rain takes the blood back up, letting it dye the clouds and droplets into an apocalyptic red.

She moves closer to me. With one hand around the back of my hollowed out skull and another on my crotch, she pulls me tight against her, opening my lips with hers, each of us trying to see whose tongue can reach the other's heart first. The fingers from her other hand are around my cock, already wet with the red rain. I don't even tell her I'm going to cum. I can tell by the way she dropped to her knees that I can forgo such porn star shenanigans. Her mouth is wide open and awaiting the shot, the exclamation point for her expression. The ejaculate hits her face. It corrodes the skin away until she is nothing but headcheese with blue eyes and ebony locks, a sex doll made out of ground beef. Her tongue shoots out of her swollen mouth like a reptile's, right through the center of my throat and into the sky. The red rain flows down the crease of her tongue, a scarlet rivulet right through us.

It boils and melts us, all the flesh and bones we hold in vein. We can feel each other disintegrate, our bodies melting in unison. We congeal into a belching clay that bubbles and sizzles as the now acid rain keeps pattering against us, now an amorphous blob devoid of any detail. The ground around us slowly breaks off into sections. We slip down the sides of one of these tar towers, swallowing it like a condom. A hole at the top of this foundation slurps us down, now a liquid being sucked through a gravel tunnel.

PEACEMEAL: THE FINAL CUT

Finally we hit bottom as a thinning putty making its way to the earth's core. the lamp casts on the ceiling resembles a corpse salvaged from an explosion. Sex undefined, it's bones, fluids, skin, and guts now part of solid sculpture of ash. It only lights one corner of the room, and not that well.

I shut it off, but the streetlights cut through the blinds, creating jail-cell silhouettes. A piece of the wall is moving across from me, cut out to look like a rodent. It moved the same way, hugging the wall, stop and go jerky motions like a squirrel. A similar creature brushes against my arm quickly. Another on the other side. I rose from the beds and saw rats all over. They swallowed the room with ugliness, fat fur bellies and tails naked of hair. I jumped from the bed to the bathroom only a few feet away. I turn around and see the floor. Hundreds of mouse traps. Some had captured the rats, necks snapped, bodies stiff as 2 x 4s. I swipe a much larger rat off my chest before it can go further.

I go to take a shower. I pull back the curtain and I am hit with warm steam air. The windows are already fogged, giving birth to beads of condensation and the paneled walls. I hear faint moans from another room. The fog fucks my pores until they ejaculate salty drops of water. I peep around the corner. Steam is rising from a little pool of rocks as water from the ceiling hits it.

The steams pulls back to reveal fifteen to twenty women, naked, covered in blood, each one wrist deep in the other. Different pitches of scream are attempting to shatter my eardrums. One frequency works, as I can feel blood oozing from my ears, thinning from the sweat. The women appear to be Japanese and Filipino with porno bodies and wet black hair hiding the careful details of their facial features.

I'm never tempted to interfere with their performance. I turn away to find a murder of crows greeting me, swallowing the house with rough blackness. I could hear the walls choking on feathers, their tongues being ripped out by the ravenous birds. The alleged soul carriers poured through windows broken by rocks, dead rodents, and other weapons and feed that they gathered. Shredded by their talons, shredded even further by the glass.

My bare feet pressed against the ground, covered with sticky layer of phlegm-skin that caught the black feathers, the white , the shit, the gutted field mice, the beheaded baby rabbits, and the eggshells still slimed in afterbirth.

My front door was ripped off its hinges as a seemingly endless stream of crows and ravens flew in, cloaking the innards of my home until it was a flinching shadow, a shrieking black hole. I backed into what I thought was a wall, but turned out to be a shallow vertical pit. I made my way back up to find myself facing a wall of beaks.

They all opened at once, like some garden of blooming flowers.

They opened so wide that the skeletons of the birds jetted out, as if they had grown sick of the scenarios. Soon the birds were boneless breasts, the solid blackness now broken up by light brown skeletal cream. The skins became so soft that I sank into them like they were tar, sinking into nothing.

------------------ steel-pipe. bodies to car. coated in oil. chloroform. hair stringy. rag over face. crease in back against lead pipe. limp and folded into ground. cradled. jammed pipe in mouth, teeth down throat. pulled pipe, mouth mangled. Coughed shards of teeth. spat. head hitting door. all fours, fingers in mouth, running over mutilated jaw. kicked in stomach, stomped kidneys, remembered chloroform. put over mouth. gathered girl. threshold. tying wrists and ankles with duct tape. cataracts. dry place. gash of pulp, guts in stalks. scabby fishnets, pinking shears. digestions. Gullet circuitry. Phallus locks.

There's a skeleton of a wind making the thick mop of hair move, the light brown tentacles of curls wrapping themselves around a white flower, the stem tucked into her ear. The house in front of her, its painted skin bending upward, revealing the brick and wood innards, collapses into itself. Her head is down as she turns to face me, curling up into a ball, her feet still on the ground, the white skirt of her dress tight as she hugs her
 knees, resting her head on top of them.
Suddenly there is an eruption from the missing foundation behind her, black fountains that begin to rain down sickly green volcanic ash and slivers of yellow glass. She stands, her shadow burning itself into the ground.

She walks toward me, her footprints leaving smoking craters in their wake, as if the ground was ice and her feet were heated coals. Her shadow is burning my skin, bypassing blister to blacken the bones. black water. human/shark hybrids. Gills melded into flesh, faces eerily fixated on nothing and elongated with sharp Sardonicus grins. acidic tongue, sexual frustration, anatomical pageantry, tin- husks. look to faces and nothing but lacerations.
 engine, wet. auto wreck. removes veins. grotesque, gravel throat, rides dwarf around burnt sticks. turd burning. opaque.
 ash. crater on shoulder. tarp, moisture. chalky flakes of flesh, cold sore, chromium. mine-field, peroxide flood. battery acid.

Centipede crawl out of mouth, encrusted with mascara. bukkake. cut off wings, slip out of skin, harp radiator. gash of atmosphere. cough up venom. spine, dog ejaculate on communion wafer tongue. hairs plucked from areola harden nipples. gash naugahide. Ziplock makes come harder. assisted masturbation. sips from needle, wades in spoon. scrap metal lodged in throat, next to moth cocoon and red shoelaces. lynched bodies dragged by trucks. naked body. handfuls of ass.

I was caught by my father talking to myself loudly about

Coprophagia. He says he does that all the time. "Which one, talking to yourself or eating your own shit?" I think. masturbation by fetus, waxing dome with bandana. melting man. cement mixer wrists. grains compacted into skin Naked in front of computer. saws, spinning chains cauterizing. waves of liquid

PEACEMEAL: THE FINAL CUT

paper. girl smiles sores on cheeks, scabs. kid digs fingernails into dogs eyes. wolf meat inhale child to waist, sucking on tubing of intestines. Child slimy, veil of wax. saran wrap overhead. pig. butcher knives. Tongue. taped hands in chests. greased junk. gaping head wound temple. mercury in tubes. flower over gushing wound. rose of brain. freshly raped. unzip flesh from heads. Aluminum foil. old woman's face backwards. ate neck. tongue taste throat. rat skull toes. trowel blades in hands. vagina tool. breathing piss at foot of bed, covered in electrical tape. Teeth in mugs. Swallowing teeth. corpse hits highway. burst out of hollowed crabs. Silk gloves emerald dress, a wig of fire, fishnets, jack boots…fevers. septic shock. Innards rung out . pond of diarrhea. bulb ceiling, long, flat, white.. coiled horses. lung-fog whirring noises from long glass. scalp. catheter bag . eviscerate skull sockets. Gash muddle. severed knees. incarnate. black market haunts. copperheads in tall grass. nasal cavity shellac. bloated dog-cunt. roach abdomens over eyes. Locusts click together like toy blocks into copper skirt. cutting at waist. Chopped in half. fly out of mouth, wings knock teeth out of head. bloody holes in gums, exposed nerve endings. Garrote telephone wire, hail clay, garment bandages. disintegration. Yellow planes in the shape of joker grins float below the purple curtain, creating smiling lacerations. breath, laughter, and lash. ball of fire and a chain of bone. cutting into wrists. saw blade.
 vein in dirt. thawed skin .translucent soil. peels skin off back. moths gotten to exposed jaw. shell fists crash…
 stalking broken carousel, dragon flies gather around wounds.

hanging from tree. razor wire wrapped around throat. ribbon, plunging knife into gut. Exploding cradles. dressed skull in chain mail. sewage. children arms. Charcoal placed on tongue. coiled intestine in corner of room. moat of dried blood, shit spewing. rectal, colonic. ash tray, pregnant. sparking rain, ejaculation from woman's mouth. eyelids split, beady pupils. ocular areola. smile wrinkled skin. crevice. Witch chin. skin melted off, skeleton of copperwire and coat hangers tightly wound, joints of lumpy clay, worms pretending to be veins. orgy of maggots where heart would be, hands peeled face.

sheet of visage, a scalp of angel hair, rotted. skull cylinder. beige worms, growing teeth at burnt end of filter. lower intestine pulled through hole in skin. wrapped around wire.
 cottage-cheese. carving tools. parts hair with straight razor, orbs of wound. hooks. wigged dead. horses slipping out of skin. rug of dead horse flesh caught in hot wind like rawhide kite, bones and guts topple to dirt, sawdust soaking disembowelment. Girl wears gown, twine coming out of waist, connected gun-metal, augmented ashen tits. skinny hands grab twine. cut. slips out of gown, frail body, skin tight. ribs break.

Blowjob cough drops. Monoliths. cinder block. extension cord ties wrists. kicked into water. twelve-year old raped 208 times. grabbed neck. thrown into brick. punched in liver, vomit. sharpened nails sliced neck. gills. sliced face, flaps of skin hanging onto muscles. sock full of stones. cupped cock and balls. testicles look like silver balls shoot out of sack like vegetables in

PEACEMEAL: THE FINAL CUT

wet grocery bag. cock mangled, hollow and pink. insect crime scenes on ceiling, pixie wings and bones crushed
 under soles of feet. pink zits. clay. steel wool. load of saliva in mouth, gobs of mucus…

I've been driving in my green car for hours, the needle on the gas gauge inching closer and closer to the red line at my left. the windshield is cracked from where the hand hit, blood on the glass as if it were shot in the chest. I can see a damp flap of skin wrapped around the hood ornament.

The metal from the ornament peers through a small oval-shaped hole, a thin brush of hairs over it.

A face, crinkled on the tip of the chrome.

The red light goes to green. they look like life savers without
 the holes. I can hear a loud scraping behind me. I look out the back window and see a trail of blood being left by the car. I turn my attention to the road in front of me, but just a quick I turn to the back again. the window is now blacked out by a figure of gory shredded flesh.

The figure cracks the window with its knee cap, torn, scraped and exposed by speed and gravel. A hand reaches around the seat and grabs my throat. It's void a middle finger. the bones stick out, unbroken but revealed. the corroded looking tip of the index finger is pressing into my neck, to dull to be painless. the figure can only make sick curdling sounds as speech is attempted, like someone gurgling on expired milk. thick bubbles of blood trying in vain to hold in the hemorrhages were around the neck and mouth to coincide with the sick sounds. the chest had been reduced to a pulpy mound. the jaw had been cracked down the middle, split in half. it hangs lifelessly on the face, held to the head by strings of muscle and skin. Saliva dried into a white crust on the mouth and tongue, which hung out of the raw hamburger face like a neck tie of meat.

I hit the break. the index finger leaves my throat. the figure grabs the crumbled flap of skin on the ornament before joining the glass droplets on the ground. the fog still halts where my window used to be. the figure is near lifeless in front of me, crystalized by the glass. I hit the gas. I watch the head pop off like a doll part, victim of a fire cracker. it disappears in the fog. the rest of its body lies crumbled on the ground. a little old man comes out of the red car, holding what looks to be a
Halloween mask, a latex zombie face in a wig of grease black stringy hairs. I get out to see what he wants. tears and confusion shrink-wrap his face as he holds up his gore toy; the mask is missing half of its face. it's lower jaw is split, the right half crushed nearly to dust, the left half completely gone.

---------------- organ grinder throws skull. starvation. bleached from inside. Capillary concrete.
Semen stains on sweater. gutted deer. headdress of posies. bullet hole egg shells. candle wax with teeth marks in it, lighting way for exit wounds. Bone paste. Dark pink clay. the jaw relocated to cheek, teeth dug into chest. urine given off cigarette smoke.

PEACEMEAL: THE FINAL CUT

Penknife ornaments. licking gates, vomit, brain shards jammed in ears, duct tape and copper wire. mummified.

Salt-water beaded body, clammy skin. blacktop. surgical knife into neck. blood spray face. smashes brick into mouth. tied up, arms over head, wrist locked rope from hook. skin road-mapped with cigarette ash, canyons of patterned blister. mouth gagged with brick, broken in half. hammer. connects with jaw, removes gag, toothless wound mouth. cunt-viscera. masturbate into guts, maggots. semen confectioner. ejaculating. gun. Cum routine. neck hollowed, split in half. legs jittering in doorway, blows to temple with handle of gun. mallet into melon. arms stretched out . screen door swinging, white metal snapped. rope-burns around neck. flannel shirt; chunk of forearm, knife in breast. curdling. hobbled to door, blood spurting out of mouth. scalped, craned head to open wound on throat. revolving door. butterflies explode through guts. oil coats tongue from back of eyes. Tatter. shards of glass on strips of paste, violin collected dust leaves clouds when crashing into face. rape scene studio audience. cough residue, sliding wet fingers across brows. lizards. broken jaw tooth mark. burn victims. cooked skins to crude cheese, plasmatic fluids. father, mother, daughter who is holding cat. five minutes.
Father shoves Mother into wall, vertical crack. daughter still holding the cat, kicks father in testicles, cough up phlegm.

Father curled in fetal, choking mucus vomit blood, daughter flips cat, stomach facing. daughter rub crotch gently, scratches up arms and fingers with claws. daughter looks down at cuts orgasmic plunge head into cat's erect cock. sucking off cat, writhes. rabbit on fire. cat scratches face. face bleeding, mouthful of spunk dripping around lips. father and mother. opposite sides of daughter, grabbing an arm. spits spunk into eyes. grabs face, father gripped daughter's arm, tosses aroused cat onto face, cock slipping past father's mouth tickling throat. cat tight around father's head, hugging face. daughter laughing fingering, sprays torrent piss ejaculate onto father, cat fucking face. daughter's knees buckle. mother, blind from cum, grabs daughter throws into ceiling. daughter hits florescent lights, fall to the ground. splintered plastic, mother rips cat off father's face punts out window. mother and father licking faces, collecting in mouths blood and cum. daughter. holding florescent light bulb. runs, screaming Japanese cartoon. smashes bulb across mother's eyes. father and daughter point and laugh at mother, rub shards from under eyes. father punches daughter in liver, keel over and vomit. down on fours, father rips pants off . daughter's head between legs, cock resting on nape of neck. wraps arms under, lifts up until head is between legs. mouth on vagina, cum grip, drives into broken glass. mother bashes bulb into back of head. arms around waist. clutches cock and balls on top of daughter, neck-trauma and orgasms. jazz hands. picks s hair out of teeth. crown shadows, splitting triangles. milk tips over glass. girls discipline of gestapo... virginal forms of budding chests, small of backs. Abominations. curtain. lazily raping. field of blenders, diced guts patter scarecrow coat. stapled to boards. Stalks of hay through potato sack. hay stuck in staples.

Coprophagia is the technical term for eating shit. Some say mother dogs eat the shit of their pups to protect them from predators. Sometimes they eat the shit of other animals, seemingly unoffended by the taste. When dogs became domesticated, Coprophagia became something of a concern among their owners. To correct behavior they found disgusting (not necessarily unhealthy), the owners tried various products to keep the dogs from munching on their own shit, like putting meat tenderizer in their food. The tradition of walking dogs may have spawned out of the revulsion owners had of their dogs Coprophagia. If the dogs shit outside, away from the home, then the dogs can't get to it.

There are these groups of adults around here, plastic gloves loose and rippled like second skin about to be shed, that collects the piles of dog shit coiled around parks and ponds and eats them.

The more extroverted Coprophagist will eat the shit right out in the open, pushing it through their front teeth with their tongue. For them it's a show, merely an gross out act. You could call them "Coprofasionists", as the more elite shit-eaters have often done so in message boards and chat rooms.

The Coprophagist more serious about his hunger, these elitists, will quietly take the shit home and cook it in any number of ways, fried boiled melted into a stew grilled etc. They swap recipes, gather for stinky little conventions, and remain in their own shitty little world not bothering anyone. They loath the extroverted ones for cheapening their lifestyle into something hollow and fashion oriented.

She was a girl just like any other within the bracket..

Hair dyed so many times the original color had been long forgotten. Face hidden behind make-up so thick it congealed into a milkcrust of a second skin. A cigarette dangles from her mouth, light rings of artificial crimson lacquer painted on the filter. You could never tell if she was wearing a confidant smile or a defiant sneer.

She had manipulated her figure via crash diets and speed pills for most of her teenage years, and the habits sleazed their way into the young twenties she currently found herself a part of.

She condemned the sexual acts of others through cries of "whore" while participating in the kind of aggravated coitus that Peter

Sotos calls a muse.

One day the girl woke up to sharp stomach pains that quickly turned into a riot as it went beyond womb.

On her mattress a thin trail of blood darkened stripes into the pink satin and lace, a dog-dick red river flowing from the canals of her vagina. Something began clawing and tearing at the vaginal walls. She screamed and passed out as her crotch began to tear.

PEACEMEAL: THE FINAL CUT

When she came to a woman was standing over her. A fat hour-glass body soiled plastered with blood and menstrual fluid, bits of meat tangled in her greasy black hair, thick against her scalp and face, almost a plaster. The woman passed a needle and twine between her fingers, tying the string tightly around her pinky, leaving it pulsing and bruise-looking. She had stitched up both their vaginas.

She gazed up at this creature of nakedness. The woman was the physical manifestation of her hidden ugliness, kept in double bolted metal tool sheds for so long that it had taught it self to manufacture blood, and build itself a body to put the blood in. The ugly fat depraved nymphomaniac that she had taught herself to hide had come bursting out of her; an abortion by choice. The woman straddled her crotch, lowering her face until the lips were only inches apart. They kissed hungrily, tongues passing through teeth and meeting new throats. As they kissed, the woman took the fingernails of her right hand and gently cut the sutures sealing her vagina shut, peeling her pissflaps open to let the cavity belch. The woman grabbed the girl's hand, curled it into a fist, and shoved it up her crotch. She's moaning and riding the fist as if she was on a mechanical bull, sucking more and more of the girl's body into her womb with each gyration.

Masturbating to book on Cryptozoology. lubricant. bubble of air between scrotum and inside of leg. yeast.. nail grenade goes off into sheets of sand.

Her cigarettes look pink and smooth under these mellow black lights. The smoke almost doesn't want to leave her mouth, sliding back into the dungeon of her face through the nostrils.

The quick-glow of ash is neon, it's light extinguishing only seconds after the inhale pulls the paper back, like fingers being skinned, the muscle drying out into a dust that's carried away in a basket of wind.

Burn victims in feet of snow. chest pains. filmstrip. velvet angelic. Skin olive. face down, arms outstretched, leg eaten, wound caked excrement. porthole of septic tank. leg floating in colonic water. gobs of shit float, brine shrimp, plankton. face and belly peeking through mud . skin around boy mouth rotting away, teeth bronze. belly swollen and purple, combustion. Logs of shit trace along belly. boy stomach explodes, intestines eaten in water of septic tank, coil than evaporate. Boy hollowed out, sink. logs of shit attach to boy husk, excrement.

Sunlight, soft nape. gutters of carbon. bodies down street, sweat. rubber injections. veins black, frostbite.

Basement bathes. euthanasia incarnate. humidity curls, gun in mouth. gallows dilapidation . nooses dangling. corrosive maturing into diarrhea.
 tap-danced on rib cage. shoes filled with blood. tattered dress on the side of the road... atmosphere interchangeable. pounding steak knife into brick wall with forehead. leech appeal. carcinogens... dissecting tools, gutting mainline into ice cap tar pits. Powdered sutures, lilies.... salt envelope.

tits blackened. Hooks scrape mucus. throat chapped from silence. infanticide. gargantuan. fans cut sun, shadow gash. saw radiates, rots, and resurrects. palmed face soaks silk-whites. twitched and busted, giving birth to shards. Egg shells crowned gashes, positioned fetuses, cribbed toads. jelly guts curdled on shelf. made of ribbons, coiled rinds of meat. regurgitation. casualty. wiring rusty. water flakes of metal, feeding. eaten infant skulls. eyes fastened to sockets, root hangs in slimed vines. light overwhelming, atomic celesta. drone pierce snaking. nerve-grooves of -pink meat, saran wrap around naked toddler. light cut skin, white jelly radioactive. skin slunk away. shake. cobalt holes ripped, sucking grinding abyss. pulled, body opaque. atmosphere gashes body. sputtered sparks. loud pop of stressed bones. contact eye, jelly rubbing capillaries. alone in body. light bulb dangles overhead, child smacking. pistol and kitchen knives. independent midnight,. Vomit cooking guts, churning bile on stove. haze. nestled in pocket, ridged bulge in pants. reflection. no face. skin darkened with oil. puddles of

Rorschach on blue boiler suit. zeroed face. rifle eyes met. plunged purgatory. targets. cradling pistol. face froze. broke. blast split his head in cross. top of neck flaps skin and hair.

Body spray-painted innards of skull. cranium shrapnel. Specks of blood hit streetlight, red stars on ground, headless body. picked up pieces of brains, squeezing in palms, push through knuckles like putty. pistol womb. streets clean. windows unstained. subconscious; a light fog, ash clouds suspended in sky like vultures frozen in explosion, urine condensation. bulk of grease on white rag. Tongue disarray, glass jar packed with coins, metal and wires encased in plastic smashed face. Tilt of pinball machine. incisor flying. pained nerves. jar of coins sandwiched between palms. bleeding from both sides of skull. Propped against wall. face swollen. Spitting gore.

Garbage disposal. Pushed head into wall, blood from jar pulsing. pistol. puckered lip hole, barrel hit back of cheek. blast ripped face. tossed into window, body hanging out. skull peered through runny nose texture. eardrums popped, black streams. eye intact glassy red.. shard of glass held to throat. blood candy-striped shard. doorway. cerebral pocket pulling clipping of obituary. rape. bruises and cigarette burns. porcelain. Rape to avenge. comedy viscera, catharsis. rats race alongside.

Obituary square placed in gullet, mouth of fish. Crumbled paper tumbleweeds, concrete slabs. cricket soundtracks. Locust cream. jagged pixie. girl, 16. wife-beater, baggy jeans, pair of torn pixie wings, recital. flapping, on fire, living tower of torched flesh and blackened bones. smoke in shape of hour-glass bodied girl. locust dividing smoke into rings. camouflaged haze. ray of light shot through locust. spear. grew pixie wings. hanged itself.

This time though, she fell to the earth.

Quiet, yellow. Pianos tapping. washes pores, swims cell, mutilations. instruments swell pupils wide, curtains. soiled garbage used as

PEACEMEAL: THE FINAL CUT

tissue by girl to wipe make-up. drawn and quartered. Numbness…hospital mattress, cold beams hitting bed. tubes coming out of arms. face bandaged, ass bare against cotton sheets. Body sheathed in tissue-gown. leg encased in paper mâché, felt tipped signatures. vision blurry. visits silhouette. swab of color on table, purplegreen sludge. eyes ring colors out, arrangement of flowers. Purples, reds, blues, and yellows rot away with exhale.

Card in garden fraction. cream background with black letters emblazed; letters illegible. almost numerical. sunlight makes world into negative of self. tubes slurped into veins by lizards that push shape into flesh. raise in scaly hills that move like water long clogged in hose, move in rubber. flowers wilt, rotting into brown. gobs of yeast, thrush.

Standing are women. blistered head to toe, water-filled raised patches of flesh most concentrated on face and hair parts. Brittle greased strands. trails broken fingers over belly while women start to cackle, grotesque. sand-caked shakes grains from pale limbs, dusting cast with glitter. motheaten blue sweater with sagging breasts... hamburger-headed lizard tongued porn-type melted into earth... naked Asians from bath house, faces hidden behind icy black hair... head buried in avalanche of spiders... lovers mutilated... food of bed, face streaked with white-out and xeroxed. legs of spiders emerged from chest. Straddling crotch. wormhole face breathed in, sucking regurgitate.

Stripped paper, shadows shrink as pupils do when the first shaft of sun makes its way beyond the bleached plastic of shades. Mouths begin the flooding process in an attempt to dull the stench of breathed undeserving of the sweet nick-name

"morning", A moniker haphazardly handed out at its confirmation. Ears of brain, fluids of anatomy. Walls of skin. sawdust, salts, and acids melt organs. bitten wires.

Tongues sentient. Throats nest in stomach. Crawls on knees. Silk cuts base of spine. Legs sheathed. Asshole snags.
Taste grooves of asshole. Pry open mouth. Spreading cheeks.

Snapping globes. Scrape colon. Cunt rings. Suck ass. Probing tongue. Rub hands in cunt grease. Table body. Lathed ass in air.

Glistening tits. Silk crumbled second skin. Unbuckled. Unzipped.

Hungrily at cock. Engorged. Lips over head of cock. Draws on cock with tongue. Pinching nipples. Sloshed cunt. Scooping juices. Fastened cock. Hooks scrape prostate. Reach in throat.

Gag. Lacquering ejaculate. Rolls tongue around mouth. Collecting spittle of cock. Gulping. Drunk on cunt.
 locked in apology. flip book of impotence. curtains flap across plastic cases.
crackling bodies. skeleton jelly bulk cooked and eaten. suck air from wall through nose and blow. repeat until blue. keep going until blood hangs vapors. flesh clings tight and rips like grocery bag vegetation tumbles, splatter icing over in recirculated

PEACEMEAL: THE **FINAL** CUT

breath.. impregnating baby killer. screwed thumbs quake. climax of crime. pins blown to keep wounds from sealing shut. hollow gruesome. millennial pinned to breast. scope slimed in scumhole resin. tamps and pads blue veins forking at knuckles. willed to cough. hiss of syndromes. genital-amputee hiding in masturbation. whirl-pooling mould rings three fingered fist. annihilation's wake, housebroken ash on cradles of infant hands, pocking wood-chip skeletons. piggy-backing leech nurse. sudden cruelty. Scarab malignancy. teeth of wrench down over rib, shaved to razor bone. held to heart. sewing needle to throat. rim cauliflower. trimmed in sick orange. floronic rabies. blown up into guts, camouflaged in sulphur. playacting Eucharist mashes brown soot between toes. standing in street. crowds meat pass. nude except for boots. Gun cylinders. firing into crowds, spinning circles of gravel platform. machine whir detonations. Crib death. cinder children.

Clouds scabbed glass sperm foetus belly... accident.... disgraced actresses vomiting lipstick as she is plastering heart slash.

Carved posture. Revisiting nausea. tapping mutation. girl ate skin out of spray-painted bath tub. covered in welts. drains chemistry. Tented fingers aching. indigestion pool. drown. puke frames screaming face. body dissolves in stomach acid. brought to mouth, reflux webbing lips. Bang head on slanted rafters. animal coughing hell. Entrails overrun with snapping vermin.

Scissors spark bone paper, cooking mouldy skin hiss of weeds.

N. CASIO POE

Smoking bruises. struggle marks. Tack statues overlooking gangway. Chopping ten pounds of chicken. Took big swallows.

Consumed obsession. dislodge. nurse slathered in glass, drying off bathing tonic. cold saunas. Sleeveless hustlers mummified in different colors of saran wrap. powder from sidewalk.. Fetish gender killers born screaming out of skull, blue milk crate full of cigarettes. Human furniture jam giant stick into piles of garbage bags. blur of flesh spiralled in limitless descent, dripped off the sides. Encouraged by rejection. Mildew influx concentrated into one indecipherable mass churning lagoon stomach. Fibre glass cuts up insides.
Shingles landscape.

Sentient condition. A machine in every possible way. Grey brain becomes illuminated; splashes wax through the screens. Vines wove themselves through the skin. Budding dolls hung from moss covered rocking horses bellow down toward blue ground. Saturated to the window with massive puppets tossed into giant shredders, leisurely meandering through eventual demise. Ripe silent throat. Spay cult medic gasping for air. Stalking catatonic mother, absorbed with chalk paintings. Sweeping valley of rayon mess. Long shadows converged with low fields, dual movements slow and choreographed. pregnant crow lay white furious in hot concrete. Neuter search parties of slashed nymphs fire walk on kitchen table, slopping cruel injury. I want the child inside of you to suffer. Watch the tiny black body be thrown against a tree. Womb blossomed industrial pastel, beautiful young violence poking through the wrinkled spawning. Raspberry man. Rodent man

PEACEMEAL: THE **FINAL** CUT

evaporates. Twins jumping into black water. Faces wading. Chins elongated. Blood pouring out back of head. Car crash victims pulled by strings to sky. Wrangled and stockpiled in underwater caves. Laughter in place of dialogue. Water purple from blood.

Sewer main spring. Cocktail dress. Ripped stockings. Skull of hair. Matchbook dentures. Lips plucked abscess. Floating ribcage. Choking eels. Tacks. Black eyes. Sculpted lust. Teeth curtains. Short hair frames. Unwraps white pouch. Cock gasping.

Twitching cocks. Flicks tongue. Pulse upward. Movements of mouth. Opens mouth. Propping tip on tongue. Hands free. Swallow cock. Coating saliva. Hits base. Close lips. Sucking slow. Bobs on cock. Dead in eyes. Pulls mouth. Gasp. Trailing thread of drool. Binds cock to tongue. Leash. Rolls tip around circumference of head. Chewing. Grabs back of head. Fucking face. Cum. Pulls cock out of mouth. Spits on hand. Masturbates cock. Demanding cum hit mouth. Torrent lobs open mouth.

Dropped. Broke. Violated. Sidewalk hit. Children's toes frostbitten. Recounting awful things. Old world scent of gasoline. Teenage lovers. Phone sex. Paper despots. Naked brushing. Spitting unapproachable beauties. Gritted teeth. Dead tear eyes. Disposable synthetic sheets. Emergency treatment wards. Benches of penitentiary dining halls. Clenched teeth.

Carved spray painted holes. Coded. Prison bricks. Sheltered.

Tongues. Appetites. Caresses and pleasure. Wreaked. Showing

bodies. Arbitrary drone. Attic. Ailing. Shaking hands.

Dismantled power boxes. Tooth nail knife. Tear gas. Underground network. Illegal abortions. Religious fanatic die in shame.

Massaged shoulders. Tore primordial fragments. Huts. Plastic sheeting. Beaten horseback. Tense. Smuggled. Lied with clean conscious to homicide detectives. Adrenaline of barricades.

Servile and craven. Sacks of broken glass. Collected food from trash. Sick dying tight.

Wreckage shouted.

Danced in shackles.

Smuggled gauntlets. Silence. Starvation. Subjugation. Bomb hearts. Ruins. Constraints countenanced. Captivity. Gilded in capillaries.

Chest wound stuffed with twigs. Fist in throat goes flat. Clenching just when turds rope over palm. Clad in bandages. Opens trunk of car. Filled with food, eggs, milk, assorted slosh. Rolls in it. Bandages absorb moisture and change color.

Sweat. oil on hair. Greasy curls plastered to forehead.

Plastered on pillory. Thin rope runs across part in hair. Pulls stainless steel hooks in nostrils, creating snout. Blood crusts the holes. Mouth held open with speculums. Screams. Lips hike up. Browning teeth.

PEACEMEAL: THE FINAL CUT

Heavily veined eyes. Pupils shrunken to pinpricks in flash of camera.

Underdeveloped child. 16 inches high. Teeth in a straight line that flattens mouth. Genitals concave after father tucked them up waist during process of molestation. Testicle busted from scrotal sack. Hanging gun metal eyeball. 9-year-old autistic missing inside bedroom of cockroach-infested apartment. food, trash soiled diapers on the floor. clothes soaked in urine.
Ever scrape the philm off your unwashed tongue then suck it off your fingernails? Has the consistency of applesauce. I think. It's been a while since I had applesauce. Has a third hand smoke taste to it… the scent smokers give off when they never wash their jackets. The forth that accumulates after you finger-fuck a slightly overweight welfare mother with teeth like sun-streaked headstones and the graveyard halitosis to match.

The breath infects everything, from its texture to its color.

Nicotine menstruation. Ash-ing labia. Clitoral filter. Cigarette birth canal. A tumor with a cord to supply its sustenance.

Cerebellum guano. A man who is most certainly a heroin addict is yelling at his girlfriend over the phone at the library. Dream of shitting dead tapeworms into a toilet. They are large and covered in tiger stripes. Homeless men hold guns to the faces of children whose intellects have been rendered inert by hours of video games… retarded developments inhibiting the truth about the limitations of their feigned toughness. Pile after pile of light calorie cows are stuffed into bags and slid off counter tops.

Acid reflux stage freeze. At the foot of the bed with chewed rats in his hand. Sacrificial offerings in silhouette.

Oscillating. Innards grooved from salt. Photographed just before carotid hosed profile. Loved with the cruelty of strangers.

Pumped on all fours and grunting and barking and cumming with throat alone. Sleeping in car with bag over head. Hammer taps on windshield above head. Caffeinated marrow. Features of vulva.

Early childhood messages. Fallopian secretion. Penetrate cell.

Eyeing all night. Clad in white. Angelic shimmer. Starless midnight. Crotchless. Kiss slow. Gliding bodies. Lapping pussies. Simultaneously finger fucking. Lost in wetness.

Fondling in the shadow twin eros casts over body. Remove fingers from pussies. Tongues touch between glazed hands. Crawl. Asses in air. Sets of eyes fastened on hard cock. Lay heads on lap.

Licking shaft. Rolling over head. Trading blowjobs. Meeting to kiss at pisshole. Swallows flesh. Savors other saliva. Ass in air. Legs spread. Soaked cunt. Strap on. Eaten from clit to asshole. Muffled moans reverberate on cock. Raise higher. Fucked with strap on while sucking cock. Tip against cleft. Rubbed cervix. Slides.
Fucking. Grinding. Keeps cock in mouth.

PEACEMEAL: THE FINAL CUT

Pressure. Pulls out cock. Screaming. Smack ass. Pull hair.

Thrust. Cums on strap on. Orgasm from guts. Shoved down on bed.

Continues fucking. Anus at the whirlpool. Lead walls. Cum webbing lips. Tear up. Tear.

Grains from sewer pipe. Sewer pipe made into dart blower. Over-muscled model's face discovered under featureless rubber mask made translucent in the sun. time lapse footage of drained pus being deep fried until reduced to individual carbon atoms.

Fart bubbles on cock pulled out to the foreskin dribbles alcohol down crack of ass falls around shaft cleansing diarrhoea specks regurgitate white spittle cools whiskey burns pupils seer to pinholes in marbled iris singes pubic hair smells like paper lit with lighters then blown out cum spewing like sketch comedy vomit gag industrial lends itself to creepy old man vibe more powerfully than most they could've been his children now grandchildren well maybe not his since he never moved beyond trailing DNA on bush prickers at neighborhood watch meetings she's still out wondering if her rapes continue while jailed in an astral plane what if any ticks she has be it spitting or shitting or lactating or leaking mucous from pipe cleaner sinuses if she willed all of it by endlessly fighting with mom if its penance for never wanting children pumping fetus eroding pills into toxic shock uterus until hot pink mess poured from vaginal aperture if she'd love for this to render any child rearing inert

N. CASIO POE

Clothes cut with scissors. Frayed seems like small tentacles. Blue cream inches away from rigor mortis pall. Salt water clumping brown hair. Breasts sloughing under arms. Insects cocooned under skin. Wet dirt excreted from the worm of her throat. Teeth the color and texture of an old man's toenails; thick, long, nicotine damage yellow. Marbled eyes like ribbon candy Rorschach tests; bright
red swirling in off white, never
 blending
together.

----

are you hearing me, pig? I hope so, cause I'm gonna talk like you're not listening. I heard that in some shitty song.

Probably some fucking garbage you think is deep, cause you're fucking stupid like that, pig.

You had it all figured out, right? Taking without giving.

Rolling over your own shit. I'll bet you love it. You fucking animal. You fucking piece of shit. I can see the faint brown coloring that stains your old skin. See it being pushed through the gaps in your rotting teeth.

Old fucks call and scream into the phone, ending on a "please?" as to render their belligerence polite. I hate them almost as much as I hate you, pig.

Palming turds like a vibrator. Roll it like dough and fuck your ass with your shit, pig. Smack your ass so big brown handprints stain the slow sliding meat, pig.

PEACEMEAL: THE **FINAL** CUT

You probably think it's not your fault.

You probably think it's all you can do.

You probably think it's out of your hands.

You probably think it's your choice.

You probably think you're allowing this.

You probably think being degraded is empowering.

Shut your fucking cocksucker, pig.

Some people just like to hurt. Some people just want to get fucked with the sort of fuck that fucking destroys the fuck out them, pig. Some people like to be pulled apart, left in fucked pieces, and put back together in no particular order. There's nothing empowering about it, pig. That's its appeal, you fucking moron.

You only know who you are after you've been hurt violently.

Forcibly.

Fucked violently.

Forcibly.

Are you fucking getting this, pig?

I love watching someone get hit, pretending it doesn't hurt them. Pretending it's what they want. Pretending it's making them cum. They reveal everything in the showcase of the paces.

You know they come completely apart, emotionally and psychologically dismembered, when the curtain goes down, the lights go off, and they know no one is watching them. They taste their own ass on their tongue. They feel the shit-philm form at the top of their throat. It flavours every meal they have. Every cock they suck. Every cunt they lap. Every day they are what they eat, pig. Shit.

Pig.

Tattooed young Japanese man strapped to a chair. Every one of his limbs is fitted with ornate halos. A thin woman in black lingerie and one opera glove stands behind him. She cuts out the left side of his skull and proceeds to pinch and fondle his brains. his tongue is affixed to a small board with an long skinny nail. She hasn't been dead this whole time. It happened before we got here. And she is no more or less important than anything else mentioned. It's not that we don't care… it's just that she has nothing to tell at the moment. She's resting.

Letting her holes close. Her skin seal.
Welts drain. In place.

This one time I did some bumps of coke off of the bulk at the base of my thumb and methodically shaved every hair off my body. I then put on a pair of fishnets she once let me use to tie her up during sex. Periodically I use them as a fuck toy, tightening them around the base of my cock and bursting a

PEACEMEAL: THE FINAL CUT

quite stinging burst of cum into the feet of them. they have never once been washed. Testicular grease falls into stains that take the form of invisible continents that peek from under the shallow black water of a leg-shaped earth. The densest of the stains is the clumpy white one carving out the circumference of the crotch, from when I would rub over it to slicken the vagina.

They must be at least two years old by now.

I get nothing sexual out of this. it's a callow mockery of performance art for the warped and tinted reflections on the surface of my television screen.

If they knew what I was doing here… what I was thinking at this moment… would they be able to process the image in a fashion befitting the nature of the act?

Flushing in the ears; in one corner a mint green lacquer and another corner gun metal blue. Brushed over clean skin of a forearm peeking from an ovular gap in the sand. It's one season year in and year out at this time of day… in this part of earth.

Early autumn. Relaxingly cool. Patch of beach untouched by oyster shards or ruined bottles. Light hasn't cracked the horizon just yet; just slivers thinly spread as to slightly raze the dark. This is the only time I like the beach. The rest of the day it's a salt pit. Low-income families, bad food, cut feet, wave battered bodies rubbing balls of sea water out of their eyes. No cars. No 200lb specimens in 85lb bags. Just us. Night lifers drained, bagged. Don't know why this one isn't in the bag or I don't care this is all for nothing they deploy armies to find skinny teenagers shut down metropolis and he took out barely a third of what happened here but we compartmentalize we consider one life as more sacred then another I don't know I don'tknow idon;tknowidont';snkown it. lk;m ,/.l;kn mn /.,

Thoughtless thoughts. Cuffed by ankles to pig husk. New episode. Dig deeper. 4 simple words. Tear down. Monosyllables.

Decade that made. Crew of mission. Appearance irresistible concept. Shuttle limelight. Education PR. Right stuff. Explore.

Flight together. Apple for teacher. Ice cleared away. Engine.

Lift off. Challenger. An awe went into smoke. Disintegrated.

Vehicle exploded. Dead faced. Space filled with debris.

Technology turned on us. Cascading systems failure. Shattered regard. Doubt power. Never perfect. Never invincible. Management exaggerates reliability of product to the point of fantasy.

Reach exceeds grasp. Consequence for future. Way we all enjoyed.

Slip bonds of earth to touch the face of god. One wall. Sound like hammer blows. Transform lives. Looked backward. Upside down. Tail of comet. Decade. Morning again.

PEACEMEAL: THE FINAL CUT

Vision into reality.

Shaking hangover. How far can he take it. revolution for the wealthy. Moral revival. Perfect springboard. Open Olympics.

Reason upsurge. Embraced virtues. Allure of permissive society.

Before ruin. All about nostalgia. White knight movie star. Never gone away. Prosperous mom. Maybe you do. Storytelling product.

Flashback before being torn in two. Clean and fresh. Rewriting.

Mesh as never before. Increasingly run by visual images.

Some hardcore band playing in a crumbling VFW hall in the middle of the suburbs. They play no music. They just cut themselves and squirt blood everywhere. They're also nude.

I woke up at 6:30 am to take a piss. When I urinated it felt like red ants carrying a thread of razor wire out of my dick, followed by a veined purple bubble that stretched out my pisshole. I pushed it out like some grim parody of giving birth.

It had a skinny tail on the end of it. it plopped in the toilet, bobbing like a buoy. My cock looked like someone had hidden a landmine in my urethra. The urologist says he thinks it happened when I attempted to slurp my cum back up my dick at the moment I had been ejaculating. a sperm that died when hitting the air made its way back into my urinary tract, to be coated in streams of piss and come, hardening the layers until grew into something roughly the size, weight, and texture of a small handball filled with baby teeth.

She made a racist remark to a black gentleman and I told her to go fuck herself and she got in my face and asked if I wanted my ass kicked and I said I don't think you'd want me to enjoy myself and then she sat on my lap and got real close and said girls are into guys that are weird and I really wanted nothing more than to fuck her.

After practice I went outside the house and saw my car turning around the corner. Someone had taken it. a mass had gathered to watch me kick and scream. I get a call from my ex-girlfriend's ex-boyfriend. He tells me he's at the restaurant around the corner and he has what I'm looking for. I go in there and see him at a table, drunk and gigging. I call him a bunch of banal cuss words and he calls me out on my boringly profane lexicon.
I brake a glass and hold it to his still grinning face and ask him for what feels like the hundredth time about the whereabouts of my car. He leads me to the parking lot, acting like an extroverted high school "weird kid", licking my palms when I grab his face and similar. I tell him none of this bullshit impresses me. I find my car, which he has filled with VHS and cassette tapes, which I proceed to smash on the ground in front of him.

A giant black and yellow centipede that turned out to be a flock of spotted birds that had clicked together to form the shape of a such a creature. They disperse as I am pointing them out, flying to a ledge underneath our deck.

PEACEMEAL: THE FINAL CUT

A basement laboratory in a prison that turns men into blue-skinned monsters that emit powerful currents of electricity from their bodies. Someone hands me a detailed etching of several people sitting at a bar. Their faces have been scooped out.

A portrait of a beautiful girl on a beach. She is holding a giant crab and smiling. I try to show her something about the both of us. All that forms is a camera crew filming animal torture in the middle of the night. We call it "snuff porn' until one of us can think of something less redundant.

I go to flush the toilet and notice a dried turd stuck to the rim. I figure the water flowing down would push it out. It does. The turd coils into itself. It has a fanned tail like a shrimp. Three smaller ones, also with fanned tails, follow it. The first turd clogs the toilet and starts flapping, getting more swollen. I step back into the kitchen and tell my mom to check this out. When we go back to the bathroom, we find that the toilet has overflowed, flooding the floor with brown and yellow chunky soup water. At the door, there is half of a small blue shark wading in the shallow lake of shit. When it opens its mouth it looks more like a toy puppet than a real living thing.

Knotted prostate locked behind scabbed anus. A hooked rubber cylinder sands the cracking pre-scar tissue, breaking the ass open again, blood and puss coating the toy in orange liquid matter. Pumps harder… the way she had been pumped and will be pumped again. she jerks off the toy as she pulls it out. Hands sticky with pumpkin-colored wound paste.

Lifts her hand to her sneering mouth and nibbles at the flakes of scab that have been mixed into the paste like bacon bits in melted cheese. Keeps fucking. At first it was cathartic… symbolic revenge for all the cocks she had taken in all of her offering ports, but as the action wore on it become something more… an arousal both viscous and pure. In short time they drop the "dominatrix vs. bitch-boy" play acting and fall into a real fuck; no irony or pretension of sarcasm or "role-reversal" presumptions. Just two people getting each other off in a fashion that arrests them in its all-points devastation.

Pornography doesn't have to be kinky or theatrical… it just needs to be intense. Grunting. Shivering. Wordless… save for those peeking from held breaths. That seems to be where I'm headed lately.

Not that I don't enjoy the spectacle of hardcore pornography and its fetishistic off-shoots, and I still achieve some level of arousal (although it's a fairly trite level) in its viewing, but I find that most of it lacks a primal root chemistry between the performers, the peddlers, and the spectators.

Rape porn doesn't even cut it, as most of that bent plays no different from the other assembly-line erotica that has become a glut on the market, only with slightly less dulled edges. Where these "rape plays" fail is in their climax; where all involved (the "victims", the "perps", and the" voyeurs")

PEACEMEAL: THE FINAL CUT

come together in an over-pronounced mutual acceptation that what we just witnessed was in fact consensual, therefore harmless, rather than culminating in the benumbing debasement that is the crucial consequence of the niche's namesake.

Too much of this so-called "reality porn" (aka "gonzo") reeks of cynical prescription; substance-deficient anti-passions played out by bland non-entities according to the uninspired whims of the intellectually crippled, the perversely illiterate, and the undemandingly satisfied. Alleged "Alternative" pornography (as much a misnomer as it is redundant) remains the biggest insult of all the upscale fringe varieties; the same banal repetition prevalent in the bulk product, only with meaningless tattoos, functionless piercings, and a charmless "punk" soundtrack. I don't mind admitting that the women who populate these features are more in line with my aesthetic preferences, but more often than not what they are putting forth in these pictures is so weirdly devoid of libidinal fortitude that the entire affair is
 practically comatose on arrival.

In all these case, What should be a three dimensional window peering into a conjoint, unbound prurience is rendered erotically inert; a candy colored party favor for gathering lunkheads looking to nut and forget. perhaps pornography's salvation lies in where it first became currency; namely in art and literature…. Perhaps even music, where any scenario can be realized in the minds of the creators, the curators, the critics, the consumers. A more personally interpretive experience, more isolating. More satisfying.

Then again… there no real physical risk, which does take much of the bite out of it. maybe the solution is filming people who don't know they're modelling for you. hidden cameras in hotel rooms. Lens peeking into bedroom windows. Those acts can't possibly be more dull than what pornography has become, even if the performers are not cosmetically satisfying according to the narrow parameters of the public sector… even if their fucking remains clumsy and unrefined… especially if it is all of those.

We're almost there… it just takes the proper presentation.

It's been so long since I've seen you, xxxxxx. Too long. A lot's been happening. My mom's doing better. She says hello. I know you two have never met, but I talk about you so much that she feels like she knows you… I think she pretends you're her daughter in law. Heh… kinda tacky I know, but her and my girlfriend have never gotten along. That's been the other thing… the relationship has steadily been getting worse. She gets jealous of you… the way I talk about you…. She says "ohh good, more about xxxxxx" all sarcastic and shit… and the day I just lost it and said "well maybe if you were more like xxxxxx I wouldn't talk about her all the time. Maybe if you were funny and nice and warm and not such an unrelenting cunt from hell I wouldn't have to throw this consistently wonderful person back in your pinched face." But it's the truth… I hate her because she isn't you. She doesn't have your heart. She doesn't have your passion or understanding or sense of wonder. She's mean-spirited, casually cruel, and yeah, she's started to let herself go. When I met her, I saw a lot of you in her. I knew I would never be able to get you, and I didn't want to be another one of these slobbering mongoloids who is barely deserving of sharing an area code with you, let alone privy to the pleasure of your bewitching affection, so I went with her, because while rough around the edges, there was maybe a chance that she could blossom into something special later on, and the possibility that I could be on the ground floor for the arrival of the next wave of splendour filled my heart with promise. But sure enough, like the others I thought could be substitutes for you, she turned on me, stopped caring about her appearance, her health, her behavior… how can I be expected to care about someone who is too viciously self-involved to even notice what a fuck-up they are? Every woman I meet is either, boring, awful, or spoken for…. But they all have one thing in common; they aren't you, xxxxxx.

Our fleeting moments passing glances across the street, or running into each other at a record store, where I steal a glance at your perfect smile as you skirt your soft fingers across the top of the LPs, those small moments are imbued with such emotional density that it gives me all the reason I need not to swan dive off a bridge into heavy oncoming traffic. I get more relaxation, joy, and clarity out of you saying "hello!" to me than I've ever obtained from the sum -total of all my relationship experiences with women. I realize that better people than me have said some variation of all of this to you before, xxxxxx.

People who are more beautiful than me. more articulate. More interesting. More successful. People who can physically, emotionally, and intellectually keep up with what you are offering in those departments. And even they have failed to keep you to themselves, so I have no hope that I can be any less catastrophic of a disappointment than them with regards to you giving me a shot at being loved by you. I'm probably no better than all the sub-mental cretins who reduce your all-encompassing beauty to mere pornographic musings on all the vile shit they claim they would do to you if given an opportunity. I know the truth, though… they'd curl up like potato bugs if you ever gave them a fraction of the time of day. Please don't think me crude, but I can't even masturbate with you in mind, because my imagination is far too limited to process a visual of the act that could do one iota of justice to the real thing. You hear all these mealy mouthed sad sacks talking about Heaven… well excuse me, but Heaven is a clogged sewage mane beneath the grounds of a mental institution for diarrhetic psychopaths compared to the possibility of an evening with you, xxxxxx, let alone a lifetime. You might not realize it, but you have given me so much more than any god or country could ever concoct even in their most opiate-equating of lies. Everything self-proclaimed good people put so much effort in pretending to be, you actually are… without even trying, xxxxxx.

Every day the cancer that is human existence gets harder and harder for me to ignore, but thanks to you xxxxxx, it's slightly bearable

PEACEMEAL: THE **FINAL** CUT

to endure. I would say I love you, but the feeling is so strong that putting it in such banal terms is not only colossally redundant, but ill-fitting. This is beyond love. Beyond obsession. Beyond worship. Beyond devotion. Beyond subjugation.

This is fucking Possession. we exist almost absolutely within the other. Neither one of us needs a personality anymore. you erase me. and I you. and We each let the other one fill in our blanks. That's where we're at now. Without touching. Without talking. Without thinking. We pass through the confusion with all the splendid randomness of a birthed universe, reclaiming discovery from disorder so it can once again become unpoisoned by the nature-raping of mankind. xxxxxx ... you'll never leave me.

A spider with legs both the length and girth of bamboo stalks crawls up my wall. I run out to find something to trap it, but my date has already started pushing it out of the room.

The spider has morphed into a sea pig. It emits slurping noises that make me gag.

A butcher shop case nursery of living lobster/fish hybrids, each with the head of different animal. I take the one with the head of a cat because it's the ugliest and most undesirable and therefore most interesting to me. it must have been smaller than I had first anticipated, because when I went around the corner to pick it up, they handed me a brown bag, which held in it a Styrofoam cup with some orange oil dripping from under its cover. Part of a cat's matted tail peeked out and swayed gently.

Cops pinch a pair of teenage girls who emerge from woods with little mounds of coke caking their nostrils. The cops open fire on their massive bag of coke. It explodes all over the ground and turns my car snow white. It becomes mashed into the ground, sodden and packed tight over the dirt. It comes off my car pretty easily.

Empty city late at night. A woman, shapely and in her mid-30s. drunk, but in a fashion that creates a serpentine gait in her movements rather than the over-pronounced toppling of girls 10-15 years her junior. We find ourselves in an abandoned subway, trading cryptic sexual innuendos. My contact lens itches. I leave her to find a bathroom. I pick out the lens. Its tracked with black dirt. I turn away from it for a second, never noticing its transformation into a large roach.

Shopping spree in a comic book shop. Purposely searching for the most sexually upsetting titles on the rack. I find one about pop star Rihanna being put through an escalating series of rape-based humiliation. nursing home abuse. lungs steamed by bus station fumes. tenement lesions. pink flowers of attic insulation. jaded appetites. garters long as a windpipe. the validity of this smear. Dead forever by these hands. Paying for what I've never done.

They always say it was just a joke when they are too ignorant to hurt.

They always blame a mouth that ran when you smell children's blood. you wrote a "dear john", i forged a suicide note, pinched with hysterics at the lie of your rape and the nerved fortitude of your phony shame. Sensation replicant.

Pewter skin caught in a zippered graze.

I submit to the angst once greeted with insult when presented by the rest of you.

A mouthful of burnt hair. Muddy inks.

Belly length tendril. Group home yellow.

Medicine bottle candelabra.

A cutter's curtain jerk. cleaned in a bank of polished rot. A knife handle with a wrench for a spine and calcified bushes where the wool cracks the corner lid.

Attraction is an endgame. disgust was the first reason.

Breastfed from anthills. Web of singed inner mouth. Silken rectum like a cave diver's line. Every version of myself looks back at who came before and wants to be thrown from a bridge. The new avantgarde is blunt force trauma that will stun us mute.

Age is the fail-safe when the past finds you a maggot, so you don't need to know why you're hated since then.

The distress of witnessing hearts joyful to be run through by the stringed wires of those who lack their savor.

Inhaled so hard the pipes vacuumed melted rubber before any hairs could be singed. drawn to identical laps. maybe soon mock-ups will be drawn, though socket interests will never match the wagging saliva their scrapers flush out. if the inside of our bellies could crawl, no termination debates would be held. Not blackened, just caramelized. One with the kettle ventricles of a boiled heart. worming voids expand in width and height.

Multisyllabic vortexes hitched until they're a screed. if you still can't believe they will be taken from you, it would do little harm to mirror their ends. a serial number on a headstone.

Driven mad in pursuit of a fault. cadavers recalled 'cause they found a worm in their food. breathing from asshole. from a light in the blankets. A nightmare well-paced.

Chalked busts balanced on accordions of legal pads. Loathed with a whisper. playacting what will become right down to the lobbed nerves. spines piled like diced millipedes the air slurped dry. Increasingly humbled by the futility of catharsis. flooded in the moment. who cares if it's an old pain?

Laid with the density. abruptions are traced in mute…Drained unconscious.
  scald tender hollows. tonsils like a speed bag. student of humility sloshing in creamed venom. sips piss from a shoehorn. Tamped ash purple from the blood. bubbles of gold mud lifting the tripe. Seer of the first puke. Clamped down to witness the heal. Cries almond butter the disinfectant leaked.

Rattling off bores to proceed as to prolong. yellow bird skulls melt in the air of my heads. half a day in an hour waiting for influence to arrive. brain of cream wrung like a sponge. Owning up to the perversity laid out by superiors who today would be cut down by proud victimhood. their secret loathing colors rooms not even a look to avert from the faults of your existence.

Every sense wracked with awe at your putrescence. If you knew this mouth would sooner orbit wounds, i doubt the allure would be remanded.

Your throat is a power tool geyser. linoleum clitoris hisses when it breaks. your face is a semen blistered cunt. Pink froth caps a menstrual inferno. Pencilled bowls of anal moss.

Intrauterine scabs flaking into piss. snotty blood fills a crayoned womb. a foetus swirls inside every kidney stone. Incubated cherubs with greasy haemorrhoid wings and massive genital warts where dimples would have been.

Walk into emergency room. Place backpack on the floor, against a desk. Open it up. A thawed-out frozen toddler. Moves a little. Touches the top of head. Caves in. turns green before my eyes. Drops to the floor, disintegrating.

Try to remember if I checked the backpack for anything that trace the hospital to me.

Neon veins. A cluster of ulcers. As if the fat had grown a stomach of its own. knits embroidered SARs masks from old sweaters. Hocks puréed lard. Too polite to not swallow it back down. Legs rendered inert from lack of circulation due to prolonged inactivity. Behavioural stasis. Skinny and purple.

Bone, meat, skin fused into crooked near hollow stalks. Switches oxygen tanks with a cylinder of cleaning solvents. When out of breath, the wheezing sounds like a laugh track warped from generation of tape dub. Fingers twitch as if flicking an invisible bell.

Steps on syringe.

Cuts foot.

Slips on blood.

Clips back of head on edge of counter.

Laughs cause both ends are wet.

Straddling abscess like a vibrating egg. Pubic hair lances the boil. Cunt-muscles clench, draining the growth. Pus shoots up into cunt, like bukkake concentrated into one white shot.

Platinum sludge hardens in birth canal, solidifying blockage.

i squeezed some blackheads and what came out were segmented eyes, almost completely veined and sinking into burgundy stalks. each iris was the color of a different shade of human skin that i had never seen before and my own sockets were packed tight with flour that had attracted millipedes that became the roof of my mouth. they tucked on instinct when my tongue would flick, dropping and rolling down my throat only to become lodged half-way until being thrown up in yellow clouds that rained stomach acid they couldn't help but absorb.

PEACEMEAL: THE **FINAL** CUT

i cut out the letters that make up your name each time they came up on the pages of your diary. Using a pair of tweezers i found on the floor of your closet i placed the paper squares beneath each toe and fingernail. i cupped whatever was left and dropped it like confetti into your bathroom sink, which i filled with witch hazel and petroleum jelly. with both swollen hands i churned the contents until i had a blue pink sludge. I curved my dense palms to scoop out the gelatinous grime, smearing it over the circumference of my body. i hope it hardens by the time you get home.

Nudging carcass. 11pm caffeine. Visions cirrhotic. Feels like cold indigestion? Hyper-sobriety. Clarity bender. Saliva diet. Ache under cheekbone. Smiles I know are not for me. what did I ever learn? Something halts purge.

Sputter silently. Urge to break my own hand becomes increasingly pronounced within.

Psychic bruise. Aim.

Apartment. 2 married couples sleeping in main area. Young wife is taken into huge bedroom/space by older husband. Abused.

Kills husband. Turns space into independent salon where she cuts the hair of children who belong to a gang that wear homemade Halloween costumes all year round. The other couple sits down their child to watch a home movie they made. They just transferred it to 3D. Child watches alone.

The film is a younger version of the father, naked with long bars of metal struck into his skin, screaming that he's going to kill the child. Laughs while apartment dwellers are burned by fire, all of them pointing at the child.

Marrow pallets churned by drill-stemmed thumb nails where the hayseed rectum forks before the corn-yellow skulls of teeth that bricked the miscarriage rag callously rendered human by the gas it carried to term.

Every pore gaped to be fitted for a laser pointer. Gargling molten pencil lead. Beauty marks where the eyes, mouth, ears, nose, and hair would be. Violent twitching. Tabbing out throat songs. All document. Thrown on back burner. Pushed farther into back burner. Soon there is soot. Just soot. Soot becoming smoulder. Smoulder creeping into nostrils to crop-dust the varying insides, sewing rare cancers.

There isn't any such thing as fiction or non-fiction. There is the truth about what has happened or the truth about what we are.

-RVY-

RED YEAST: A VILLIFIED BLUE PRODUCTION:

yeah that's right, your humble blogger Helen Mawdhit here briefly worked in porn.

a misguided foray from Villation Books called Vilified Blue that got raided by the feds for producing illegal materials. there was always something sketchy about that place, but a job's a job and i like looking at pretty people with broken spirits and sour hearts.

there was one time when i got there early and Aevea, one of the starlets, had also arrived early. it was a semi-heavy BDSM set up for the day. we talked casually while she prepped herself. girl took care of herself, not like a lot of the other performers, who would booze it up, party all night, show up late looking wrecked (sleepless night wrecked, not fucked-like-a-nasty-pig wrecked), which meant that the shoot would get delayed cause they'd have to spend more time in the make-up chair to get them looking decent.

i never had the guts to tell them that the audience for what we're producing, the neo-raincoat-er crowd, would prefer it if the performers were a little more rough around the edges, a little grimier, but Gene Murifalt, the once great exploitation director who had taken the reins on this *Red Yeast* project, had delusions of auteur eloquence. maybe not a delusion, but a calculated persona designed to mask the more severe elements of his handler's enterprises, which we discovered included real rape, snuff, and child pornography.

none of us ever witnessed the production of those materials, he had a whole other crew for that side of the business. don't believe the bullshit you saw in *8MM*, this guy wasn't some laconic Bond villain. his mask of sanity never slipped from the razor-boned cattle skull of his true form.

anyway, Aevea and I had become friendly. she would leave and go on to some mild notoriety in more "prestige" pictures within this genre, which would then lead to some minor appearances in low-budget but creatively admirable horror movies, even becoming a respectable recording artist and a published author. this is what we bonded over most of all; our mutual creative aspirations. we discussed our work outside of "work", our influences, our favorite films and albums.

it was still a long time before anyone would show up. we discussed everything but fucking, which seemed to relieve her, as all she was ever asked about pertained exclusively to cunts and cocks. that's not to say she was bothered by the questions, or would angrily refuse to answer them, she'd just become exhausted by it.

the conversation then reached the peak;

"you wanna see what i found on Murifalt's computer?"

"sure"

Aevea leads me to Murifalt's office, which is unlocked. the computer is on. he uses a type of browsing program of which neither one of us ever heard. sort of like TOR: the browser that masks your IP address, enabling the user to explore further beyond the surface web, hitting those mystery sites that dwell like a lodger of the mind.

Aevea opens it up, looks through the bookmarks, finds this website that has his phone # on it.

the page is called "Deep Web Macumba"; an early example of a streaming porn service. on this page there are hundreds of videos, live feeds, audio clips, of graphic violence and depraved sex.

the difference between what we produce and what we found here? none of this looked or felt even remotely "staged".

let's face it, porn films are bullshit. yeah, the organ is bracing the orifice, but the scenarios and reactions are all very well-rehearsed, the climaxes choreographed. it's not about "reality", it's about getting off, and most of us get off on fiction, not autobiography. fiction strokes our ego, puts our desires right in front of us. you'll never fuck these people, and you'll never fuck this good, but you can dream it, and we can produce that dream in semi-flesh and beam it to your cerebellum's den of

PEACEMEAL: THE FINAL CUT

iniquity on a cathode ray from the mouth of a cum-face. the performers are the avatars for who you want to fuck and how you want to fuck.

what we saw on Deep Web Macumba wasn't a "performance". these were sincere reactions to the acts upon the bodies, and they were all some gradient of pure terror.

of all the clips we witnessed, one stood out the most to us; two young girls, probably underage. wall dirt and floor grime caked on their underfed sweating skins. hair long and matted, clumping in certain spots. they sat across from each other at a wooden table, strapped to chairs. their heads lolled around in a druggy stupor.

a figure comes in. gender inconclusive. the figure wears a brown rubber smock with matching gloves and a gimp mask unlike any i have seen before. it zipped up vertically from the base of the neck. over the mask was ornate headgear, an old time dental brace.

from the back of the apron, the figure produced a large machete. the figure placed the knife, handle facing the figure, between the girls. The figure then spun the knife around, waiting for it to stop. this motion was repeated until the desired result was achieved; the end of the knife pointing toward one of the girls.

camera cuts.

next scene. the girls are positioned on all fours, ass to ass.

the figure returns, holding the large knife.

the figure stands facing the camera, between the girls.

the figure holds up the knife, rotating the wrist until the blade is over the girl it landed on in the previous scene.

the figure begins to push the handle against the other girl's asshole. she makes intense gasps and hocking coughs as the handle is pushed up her rectum.

the blade is between the other girl's cunt and ass, resting on the taint.

a muffled voice from behind the camera says "BUCK'.

that must have been their cue. the girls push their backsides into each other until the knife is swallowed by them, sawing the cavities.

i wonder to myself if these girls had their colons mic'd up, cause i think i can hear their insides being gashed and pulped by the knife.

chunky, muddy blood falls between them onto the bed. the camera catches their faces; eroded nerve fatality in the teenage visages, which when inspected closer might actually be pre-teenage visages.

after a while, the cracked sound of the cutting falls into a mushy pounding. the girls eventually pass out (or die), falling onto the bed, their asses connected in the air, glued together with gore.

the camera lingers around this girl-flesh pyramid before cutting to the next scene, where the figure has returned to hack up what's left of these girls, the camera never wincing from the butcher-shop banality of this final act.

Aevea doesn't believe what we watched is real.

"It seemed too scripted, to plotted out. good FX though."

i admire her cynicism, and concede that yeah, it must have been a fraud, or some horror film project ala *Guinea Pig*, the Japanese series of mock-snuff films that, while effective, still

PEACEMEAL: THE FINAL CUT

could only exist in the realm of art. what we saw was no doubt a "production"; moody lighting, multiple camera angles, a slasher villain, sound design, stylized photography. but the reactions of the girls, the way the blood and guts fell, it just seemed too real to not be real. that didn't look scripted to me.

we closed out, left everything as we found it, and still had some time to spare before the rest of the crew got there. i attempted to ruminate on what i just saw while still sneaking peaks at Aevea. she definitely has that special something i continue to look for in adult film stars. not just being hot, but making you hot. not just making you wanna jerk off, making you want to fuck.

Chanel Preston makes me want to jerk off.

Riley Reid makes me want to jerk off with a *side* of making me want to fuck.

Dana Vespoli makes me want to *fuck*.

that last one?
that is the pinnacle tier.

----

thank you for reading this new edition of PIECEMEAL. this is for those of you who missed it the first time around, and for those of you who did manage to snag the first edition, it is my hope that you'll find this version to be maybe a bit more clear in its connections to the wider CRINGE MYTHOS tapestry (for instance... the characters have names now).

in the previous edition of this collection (published by Nihilism Revised in the late summer of 2019), i closed it out with yet another tirade from someone using the internet handle BLACKPILLAR13. whether it was RAND PROUSHAYTHE or ELMER KRUGE or someone yet unrevealed to me, i couldn't say.

upon revising the manuscript, i found the content of the epilogue to be too coarse, too redundant, and too heavily lacking in the realms of imagination and craft, so it has been excised from this revision.

all i can say is that it spoke to who i was at that time while huffing the methane of my most mean-spirited and invariably ugly of headspaces, but as i am now, i no longer find worth in such mediocre petulance... especially when that kind of ultimately source less angst is widely available after having being co-opted by dark money think tanks, whose sole concern is maintaining a status quo that benefits themselves and the increasing few who are exactly like them.

trying to be better.

GO AWAY.

```
Please remember to purchase directly from  us at
SDP:
https://sweatdrenchedpress.webador.co.uk/order-1
  to ensure we can continue putting out
innovative, transgressive, experimental and
important works.

Also, please leave a review over on Goodreads,
Amazon, or wherever you wish.
```

PEACEMEAL: THE FINAL CUT

N. CASIO POE

PEACEMEAL: THE FINAL CUT

Author's Bio:

N CASIO POE lives in Long Island, NY. His full length written works include TERSE, BARRAGE TAPES, GOREGAZE, BLUE YOLK, and GANGERS (all Sweat Drenched Press) and he has had short pieces appear in the AGON JOURNAL, USERLANDS, and DARLING DELIQUENTS (Sweat Drenched Press).

N. CASIO POE

MORE WORKS from N. Casio Poe:

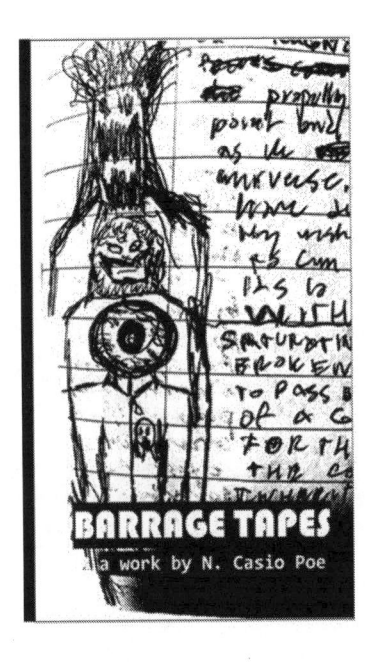

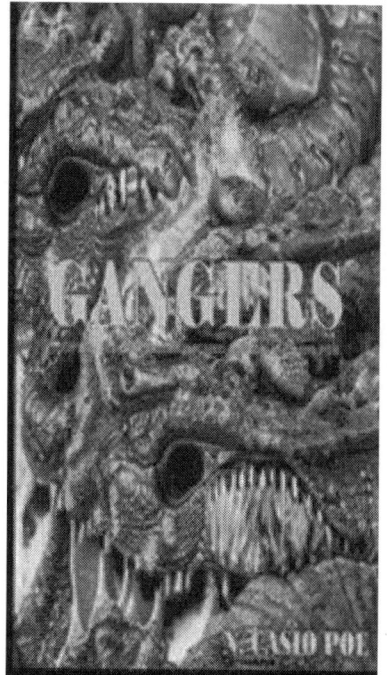

PEACEMEAL: THE FINAL CUT

N. CASIO POE

PEACEMEAL: THE FINAL CUT

Printed in Great Britain
by Amazon